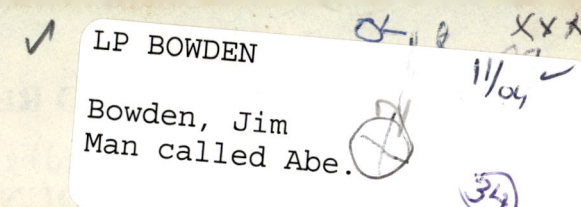

ATCHISON PUBLIC LIBRARY
401 Kansas
Atchison, KS 66002

SPECIAL MESSAGE TO READERS

This book is published by
THE ULVERSCROFT FOUNDATION
a registered charity in the U.K., No. 264873

The Foundation was established in 1974 to provide funds to help towards research, diagnosis and treatment of eye diseases. Below are a few examples of contributions made by THE ULVERSCROFT FOUNDATION:

A new Children's Assessment Unit
at Moorfield's Hospital, London.
•
Twin operating theatres at the
Western Ophthalmic Hospital, London.
•
The Frederick Thorpe Ulverscroft Chair of
Ophthalmology at the University of Leicester.
•
Eye Laser equipment to various eye hospitals.

If you would like to help further the work of the Foundation by making a donation or leaving a legacy, every contribution, no matter how small, is received with gratitude. Please write for details to:

**THE ULVERSCROFT FOUNDATION,
The Green, Bradgate Road, Anstey,
Leicester LE7 7FU. England
Telephone: (0533)364325**

A MAN CALLED ABE

The mysterious disappearance of Doug Walters, owner of the Circle C, brings a cry for help from his wife Dorothy to an old friend, Cap Millet. Cap's search leads him to link rustling with a deadly scheme for power. Greed, ambition and revenge ride the same trail and loyalties are tested to the limit in a final showdown which reveals the identity of a man called Abe.

*Books by Jim Bowden
in the Linford Western Library:*

SHOWDOWN IN SALT FORK
CAP
THUNDER IN MONTANA
INCIDENT AT BISON CREEK
HIRED GUN

JIM BOWDEN

A MAN CALLED ABE

Complete and Unabridged

LINFORD
Leicester

First published in Great Britain in 1993 by
Robert Hale Limited
London

First Linford Edition
published July 1994
by arrangement with
Robert Hale Limited
London

The right of Jim Bowden to be identified as
the author of this work has been asserted by
him in accordance with the
Copyright, Designs and Patents Act, 1988

Copyright © 1993 by Jim Bowden
All rights reserved

British Library CIP Data

Bowden, Jim
 A man called Abe.—Large print ed.—
 Linford western library
 I. Title II. Series
 823.914 [F]

ISBN 0–7089–7580–1

Published by
F. A. Thorpe (Publishing) Ltd.
Anstey, Leicestershire

Set by Words & Graphics Ltd.
Anstey, Leicestershire
Printed and bound in Great Britain by
T. J. Press (Padstow) Ltd., Padstow, Cornwall

This book is printed on acid-free paper

1

BILLINGS lay under an intense noon sun. Townsfolk escaped its white heat by staying indoors, taking their dinner hour. The staff of the stores and the bank were at their daily low.

There was no one to notice the five riders who drifted into Billings at intervals from different directions. And if there had been they would have taken little notice of an individual who did not attract attention. Their only thought might have been, 'Fool, riding in this heat.'

The horses walked slowly, held by steady hands, without a sign of nervous tension. Their riders gave every aspect of casual visitors, maybe even riding on after a drink at the Longhorn Saloon.

But to the men themselves their actions were far from casual. For the past week, riding from their camp in the hills to the west of Billings, they had studied the town and its habits.

Towards the middle of the main street lay the county bank flanked by the general store, which bore the name Scriver and Son, and the barber's shop with its red and white pole boldly signifying its purpose. These three buildings made up one block. The block to the north was occupied by Anne's Cafe, Helen Bowman's haberdashery store, and the offices of the *Billings Herald*. The block to the south was lined by seven houses. Opposite was the white painted, wooden church with its well-kept ground neatly fenced. Several houses stretched to the south before their pattern was broken by the livery stable. To the north of the church were the offices of the Billings law firm of Tyler and Manning, next to which was the stage office and the sheriff's office. The Longhorn Saloon occupied the next block beyond the sheriff's office.

Neat houses lined the rest of the main street in either direction, with only the Cattleman's Hotel intruding into their symmetry.

Every member of the gang knew the layout, could draw it in the dust blindfold. They knew which side streets gave the best access to the main street and which alleys might present obstacles. They had studied the comings and goings of the inhabitants at all times of the day and knew that at noon a lethargy settled over the town which it scarcely shook off by three.

Their timing was right.

Gil Fenton rode his horse to the rail outside the bank. The last to arrive, he took in the situation as he swung slowly from the saddle. Dutch Hardy was coming out of the church, Drew Kinkaid was sitting in a chair outside of Anne's Cafe, seeking the shade of the sidewalk's awning. When he saw Gil swing from his horse he rose to his feet, untied his horse from the rail and walked casually towards the bank. Blackie Fisher emerged from the Longhorn Saloon, climbed on his horse and rode slowly towards the church where he swung from the saddle and joined Dutch as he was releasing his horse from the rail. After a casual exchange of words they walked slowly across the street towards the bank which Gil and Drew were entering. Noting these planned movements, Abe Reynolds mounted his horse outside the Cattleman's Hotel. If everything went according to plan he should arrive outside the bank at the precise moment.

As the door swung shut behind Gil and Drew, Dutch handed his reins to Blackie and took up a position outside the bank. Blackie unhitched Gil's and Drew's horses and held all four animals, quietly soothing them.

At that precise moment a man and a woman emerged from one of the houses to the south of the bank. They were deep in urgent conversation as they hurried along the road and on to the boardwalk which started at the general store.

Inside the bank, a clerk looked up from his figures to see who had entered the bank.

"Good day, gentlemen," he smiled pleasantly. "Mighty hot day." He mopped the sweat on his brow with a handkerchief as if to emphasize his observation. "What can we do for you?"

"Jest keep your mouth shut and hand over all your cash," rapped Gil, drawing his gun from its leather.

The amiable smile vanished when the clerk found himself looking into the cold muzzle of a Colt pointing at his middle.

The words penetrated the whole room, startling the man sitting behind a desk in the railed-off portion of the bank. He looked up in alarm.

"Don't try anything," called Gil with a sharp glance in the man's direction. "Get round here and let my partner in." The man hesitated.

"Move!" rapped Gil.

The sharp tone needled the man into action. He pushed himself to his feet and waddled his rotund figure quickly to the door at the end of the long counter. As he slid the bolt free, Drew kicked the door open sending the man staggering backwards.

"You the manager?" snapped Drew, menacing with his gun.

"Yes, yes," spluttered the manager, nodding his head vigorously.

He wanted no trouble. He hated pain, would do anything to avoid it and he faced a gun which could inflict it and further still could spit death. He wanted none of it. Better to be a live coward than a dead hero. Besides, the money they were demanding was not his.

"Then you'll have the key to the safe," said Drew, stepping forward.

"On my desk," spluttered the manager.

"Get it and open up," Drew ordered.

The manager, sweating profusely,

with the heat and fear, scurried to the desk, grabbed the key and turned to the safe.

When Gil saw that Drew had everything under control, he turned back to the clerk. "Here, bag all your loose cash." He thrust a canvas bag under the glass panel. The clerk, seeing the reactions of his manager, decided against playing the hero and did as he was told as quickly as he could.

Drew watched the manager fumble the money from the safe into the saddle-bags which he had dropped on the floor beside him. "Hurry it up!" rapped Drew.

With relief the manager thrust the last bundle of notes into the bag. "That's the lot," he panted, his face red with the exertion.

Drew grabbed the saddle-bags. "On the floor, face down," he snapped.

"You too." Gil waved his gun menacingly at the clerk. "Neither of you move for five minutes or you'll be in trouble."

The two gunmen started towards the door when the commotion outside alerted them.

"You can't go in there," said Dutch, stepping in front of the man and woman who, deep in conversation, had not been aware of his presence until he blocked their path.

"Of course we can," snapped the woman irritably. "The bank isn't closed. We have an appointment with the manager at noon."

"That's right." The man backed up his wife's statement. "Out of our way."

"Not yet you haven't," replied Dutch, a sardonic grin on his face.

"Now see here . . . " the man began.

"No, you see here," snapped Dutch, poking the man in the chest and leaning forward menacingly. "You ain't going in there."

"Get out of my way young fella." The woman bustled past him.

"This persuade you, lady?" Dutch whipped his Colt from its holster and brought it to bear on the woman. But she was already past Dutch and did not see the menacing weapon. She strode on. Dutch squeezed the trigger. For one brief moment the world seemed to stand still, frozen by the explosion. Then it erupted into a maelstrom of action.

The bullet drilled into the woman's back with a force that jerked her to a stop then threw her forward on to the boardwalk. Her husband, shocked in the moment of horror, threw off the disbelief and hurled himself at Dutch. Dutch staggered sideways under the impact and automatically swung his gun on the attacker and squeezed the trigger. The bullet took the man in the chest. His eyes widened then glazed over as he tried to grab Dutch before he pitched forward into death on the sidewalk.

Abe Reynolds had timed his ride to perfection. The horror of the killings only a few yards in front of him shocked him to the core. The sight of life suddenly cut off drew a tightness to his stomach and constriction to his throat. But he was into a timed ride, one which would bring him to the bank at a precise moment. That ride did not alter.

In spite of the chaos around him, he automatically steadied his horse and kept it moving. What the hell had gotten into Dutch, slaughtering two innocent people in a cold-blooded killing?

At that moment Gil and Drew burst from the bank, their guns ready for any eventuality. Gil took in the scene in one swift glance. "What the . . . ?"
The impact of the shootings hit him. "Damn you, Dutch, you've let all hell loose now. Git out of here."

Gil came off the sidewalk and threw a bag to Abe. Drew was right beside him, tossing the saddlebags across the saddle. Their actions, prearranged so that the mounted man could make a speedier getaway than those who had to mount their horses, jerked Abe back to the action. He stabbed his horse into a gallop and was away down the main street before the others were in the saddle. He heard gunshots, flattened himself and urged the horse faster.

Behind him all hell was let loose. Dutch's shots had roused a sleepy town. The door of the sheriff's office was flung open and the lawman and his deputy, with Colts in hand, burst out in a crouched run. They took the situation in in a swift glance. Four men were climbing on to their horses, at the same time swinging them for a quick getaway. The lawman loosed off four quick shots and dived to the ground.

A horse reared. The rider tumbled backwards, lost his grip on the reins and fell heavily in the dust. The other three riders were already kicking their mounts into a gallop. Seeing their companion fall, two of them checked their horses. Immediately they were met with a crescendo of bullets as other guns joined those of lawmen. One rider jerked, his eyes widening with disbelief before he too hit the dust. The other rider turned his horse quickly, flattened himself in the saddle and yelled to his horse to run. Hooves pounded along the main street of Billings, drumming the tune of escape.

The lawmen jumped to their feet and raced to the robbers lying in the dust. The sheriff and his deputy kept their guns trained on the silent figures, making the final few steps of their approach tentatively.

"They won't trouble us any more," said the sheriff, holstering his gun.

Folks were running from all quarters, yelling to each other.

"What's happened?"

"Bank robbed."

"Hell."

"Who did it?"

"Don't know."

"Sheriff got two."

"Bastards shot Henry and Emma Sloane."

"Hell."

"Posse, we need a posse."

"Get after the others."

"How many?"

All sorts of numbers were bandied about by those who didn't know and who made wild guesses, swearing they had seen it all.

Ignoring the bedlam which approached them from all sides, the deputy glanced at the sheriff who was standing over the two bodies. "Know 'em?"

The sheriff nodded. Yeah, that's Blackie Fisher and the other's Gil Fenton."

The deputy looked sharply. "Gil Fenton? Leader of the Fenton gang?"

"None other," nodded the sheriff.

The deputy let out a low whistle. "There'll sure be a lot of folk pleased to know that."

"Wonder what went wrong," said the sheriff, glancing at the bodies of the Sloanes. "The Fenton gang have never been known to kill before. Seemed as though they wisely steered clear of the ultimate."

"Something always comes to catch up with the lawless," commented the deputy. "Pity it had to be in Billings and a pity it had to be good folks like the Sloanes." The deputy clipped the words short. "Hell, Matt's going to take this hard, poor kid."

"See if you can find him," said the sheriff. "All right folks, keep back, please keep back," he yelled as the people of Billings crowded round to see the aftermath of the upheaval which had struck their peaceful town at the laziest part of the day. "Charlie, the bodies are all yours," he called to a tall thin man who always wore black trousers and a dark-coloured shirt saying they befitted his position as undertaker in Billings. "Case, organize a posse." The sheriff stamped his authority on the situation and Case obeyed instantly. He had no need to ask for volunteers, men were already running to get their horses.

A path cleared through the crowd as a panting, redfaced bank manager followed by his shocked clerk pushed their way to the sheriff. "Did you get a look . . . ?" The words froze on the manager's lips when he saw the bodies of the two outlaws. "Oh." He swallowed hard with distaste at being confronted with the outcome of violent death. Then he gathered himself together. "My money, did you get my money?" he squeaked, looking round anxiously.

The sheriff glared at the bank manager. He was a man who always irritated him with his fussy, effeminate ways and here he was, more concerned about the bank's money than the fact that two of the most respected members of Billings' community were lying dead on the sidewalk. The sheriff was disgusted.

"Got clean away with it," snapped the sheriff. "Had a man already mounted to make a fast getaway."

The bank manager groaned and rolled his eyes in despair. He plucked a handkerchief from his pocket and wiped his brow. "Well, what are you doing about it? You should be out there chasing and catching them," he squawked, flapping his arms in the direction taken by the robbers.

The sheriff tightened his lips. "There's a posse being organized now," he rapped. "How much did they get?"

"Three hundred thousand," spluttered the bank manager, as if he was afraid to reveal that he had held such a large sum in the bank.

"Hell!" the sheriff gasped in amazement. "Why the hell were you holding so much?"

"It was a transit. Came in to us overnight for onward shipment tomorrow," the manager explained.

"Here for a short time and in that time the Fenton gang hits the bank," mused the sheriff. "Too much of a coincidence to be one. Must have been a tip-off from inside."

The bank manager threw up his hands in horror. "It wasn't me and it couldn't have been anyone else in the bank. No one else knew. I accepted it myself after closing time yesterday."

"Right," said the sheriff. "Then it

must have been someone employed by the bank elsewhere. I'll want more details when I get back." He turned to take his horse from a rider who had brought it from outside his office.

Already there were twenty men in the saddle and more were riding to join them. "Let's go!" yelled the sheriff and put his horse into a gallop.

Amidst yells of encouragement the posse set their horses after him. Dust rose from the pounding hooves carrying men bent on a ride of vengeance.

The light was fading fast when weary riders rode into Billings. Trail dust covered men and horses alike.

"Get them?" Anxious questions were shot at them as they made their way along the main street and dispersed to their homes and lodgings.

A sad shake of the head, and one word, "No," told a story of frustration and disappointment.

The bank manager, eagerly awaiting the return of his money, was standing on his steps of the bank when the sheriff pulled his horse to a halt.

"Sorry, we lost their trails," he said. "They went off in three directions. I split the posse, but we all ran out of luck. I trailed the fella with the cash but he covered his tracks by using Wetwater Creek. We couldn't find where he left it. We'll go out again in the daylight but I don't hold out much hope."

He turned his horse and rode away, ignoring the profanities flung after him by a despairing bank manager who could already feel the lash of criticism from the head office.

2

SHORTY WELLS took the south trail out of Two Rivers. He kept to a steady pace for he had a long ride ahead, a ride which he hoped would bring him rich returns.

He only stood five foot seven in his stocking feet but he was broad, and muscular, his height belying his power. Life had treated him harshly but it had toughened him. A drifter, he rode close to the law and was ready to hire his services to anyone willing to pay good money. He had ridden into Two Rivers nine months ago with the intention of moving on, but a brawl in The Gilded Cage, when he had outsmarted Mel Clancey's troubleshooter, had resulted in him being offered the same job.

He got on well with the owner of The Gilded Cage and Mel figured

Shorty would be an asset in his future plans.

Shorty chuckled to himself as he recalled the brawl. If it hadn't been for that chance encounter he would have been far away and would have lost the opportunity to make a fortune. Funny the way things work out.

When his boss had hinted at a more important job for Shorty, one which would need additional riders who would be ready to use a gun if necessary, he had seized the moment to say that he knew of two such men.

Mel had agreed to his absence for eight days.

Now he rode on that mission, but he was unsure if he would find the men he sought. One of them he had last seen two years ago, the other five years ago. Maybe he was on an impossible quest, but he had to try. They were important to him on two counts, as Mel's riders and as the source of a fortune.

Four days later he rode into Boulder and took a room at the small hotel which gave the appearance of having seen better days. In fact the whole town had that air about it. It seemed as if the world was passing it by. It boasted a tatty saloon, a livery stable which did little trade and a row of half-empty houses. The sign outside the sheriff's office hung by one hook and squeaked with every movement of the wind. The door of the office had been locked since the day the sheriff gave up his job and moved out of Boulder four years ago.

Shorty saw little difference from the last time he visited Boulder two years ago and hoped the man he sought was still here.

As he washed away the dust of the long travel, he hoped the stableman had got over his surprise at getting a customer and was taking good care of his horse.

The clerk at the hotel offered him some food, which Shorty accepted but he hardly enjoyed its lukewarm texture and salty taste. He ate quickly, anxious to go to the saloon, which he figured would be the best place to make contact with the man he wanted to see.

He had spent two hours in the saloon, small-talking with the barman and chatting to the two girls who saw possibilities for the night's earnings. He refrained from asking about the man. He did not want to draw attention to the reason for his visit to a hick town like Boulder. Besides he knew the man only by one name and he was sure he would not be using it.

But after two hours he was beginning to despair. He had hoped to make contact quickly. Maybe the man had moved on, maybe he wasn't coming to the saloon tonight, maybe . . .

The batwings squeaked. Shorty glanced over his shoulder. His pulse raced. This was the man. He was still here. Shorty blessed his luck. He watched through the long mirror behind the bar as the man strolled to the counter. The batwings squeaked again. Another man moved into view. Shorty gave an involuntary gasp. It couldn't be. But he was certain it was. This was even better.

He casually studied the two men as they got their order. They drank their beer at the counter then called for another. When they received their glasses, filled to the brim, they pushed themselves from the bar and crossed the room to a corner table. Shorty noted that they both sat with their backs to the wall and faced the room. It was the action of men who were always alert for danger. From their seats they covered every angle of the room and could watch the balcony which ran along one side of the building. No one could enter the saloon without being seen. Shorty smiled to himself when he thought of the shock he was going to give them.

He sipped his beer and when he saw their glasses were half empty he drained his and called for another. He picked up his beer and walked casually towards the corner occupied by the two men.

He was only halfway across the room when he sensed a tension come to them and he was aware of hands moving just that fraction closer to their gun butts.

"Mind if I join you?" said Shorty amiably as he placed his glass on the table.

"Yes!" rapped the tall wiry man as he pushed himself back in his chair to give himself greater freedom of movement should he need to draw.

"Don't think you will when you hear what I have to say," said Shorty, ignoring the venom in the one word.

"We said scat!" snarled the broader, thickset man.

"Don't like strangers?" replied Shorty casually. "Well, you'll like this one." Shorty pulled out a chair and sat down, fully aware that a gun had been drawn and would now be pointing directly at his middle under the table. He was careful to keep his hands in sight.

"Leave us," hissed the tall man. "We want no trouble."

"That's understandable," agreed

Shorty. "Drew Kinkaid and Dutch Hardy wouldn't want to draw attention to themselves." He kept his voice low.

"Who you talking about?" rasped the tall man. "This here's Clay Evans and I'm Rick Paine."

But Shorty had seen a flash of alarm come to their eyes. It was only momentary but he recognized it.

Shorty gave a small smile and shook his head. "No," he said. "You're Drew Kinkaid," he glanced at the tall man, "and you're Dutch Hardy." His glance turned to the thickset man. "And you can put your gun away, I ain't a lawman."

"I'll leave it where it is just in case," replied Dutch, his eyes darkening with a caution thrown at Shorty.

Shorty leaned forward on the table. "You're entitled." He smiled. "Just so's you don't go on denying who you really are — and I know I've identified you both correctly — let me tell you I was in Billings five years ago. Saw it all happen. You Dutch pulled the trigger which caused the upheaval by killing two innocent people. You'd have all got away with it if you hadn't been so hasty." He saw Dutch stiffen. "Drew," he turned his eyes on to an intent face, "you came out of the bank, threw the saddle-bags, which I figure must have contained the cash, to the horseman. Don't know his name, must have been fairly new to the Fenton gang. Having him already riding was a smart move, enabled him to get clear with the cash before all hell was let loose. You were lucky, Drew, to get the horses. Gil never made it and Blackie Fisher got his." He paused then added, "Satisfied I'm right about you two?"

Drew and Dutch exchanged glances and each noted that they both thought alike. This fella knew too much; it was no use trying to bluff him. Better find out what he wants and then deal with him.

Drew eyed Shorty and asked, "So, if we are who you say we are, what do you want?"

Shorty grinned. "Oh you're who I say you are, so, as I know you, I reckon you deserve to know who I am." He nodded sharply at each of them, revelling in the fact that he had the upper hand and knew that they knew it. "I'm Shorty Wells. You won't have heard of me. I've kicked around. Sometimes ridden on the wrong side of the law but, unlike you fellas in Billings, I never got caught with my pants down."

Drew acknowledged Shorty's information with a curt, "Git on with it, what you want?"

"Well, let me tell you a bit more. Seeing that raid, I was fascinated by the Fenton gang, especially when I heard they'd got away with three hundred thousand dollars. That's a hell of a lot of money. I stuck around until the posse came back, they'd lost all tracks of the three hombres that made their getaway. The sheriff and ten men went out again the following day but again came back empty-handed and not even a clue as to where you'd disappeared to. So that was that. I left Billings and drifted around doing this and that. I picked up news from time to time that a couple of fellas were making enquiries about a hombre name of Abe Reynolds. There were also rumours that the money from the robbery at Billings had never been found, and there were stories of a double-cross. So I put two and two together, figured the two fellas looking for Abe Reynolds were you two, that he was the getaway rider at Billings and that he must still have the cash."

"So?" prompted Drew, giving nothing away by a comment.

"Two years ago I drifted into Boulder. Didn't stay long, I can tell you, not in a dump like this. But before I left, I had a stroke of luck, well, it's turned out to be a stroke of luck, though I didn't know it at the time. I saw you." Shorty looked at Drew.

Drew toyed with his drink and Dutch still kept his Colt steady under the table.

"Get to the point," hissed Drew. "What do you want?"

"I'm coming to that, just give me time," replied Shorty. "I saw only you. Didn't see Dutch. Right, that wasn't important at the time. There had been a price on your heads, guess there still was but I ain't such a law-abiding citizen, so I drifted. Nine months ago I drifted into . . . " Shorty stopped with a smile. "Ah, well, where would be telling." He saw Drew stiffen. "Relax, Drew. All in good time. I got a job, trouble shooter for the saloon owner. One day a fella comes in. Thought I recognized him but wasn't certain. Made enquiries about him and was told he was a highly successful rancher in those parts. So I figured I'd made a mistake. He wasn't a regular customer at the saloon, but eventually he came in again. I had the opportunity to study him a bit longer and I felt sure I was right. I felt certain the last time I'd seen him he was hightailing it out of Billings clutching saddle-bags and a cloth bag."

"Abe Reynolds!" Drew and Dutch hissed the name together. Their expressions showed amazement at the news.

"Aye, but he don't go under the name of Abe Reynolds now," said Shorty.

"Well, I'll be darned, after all this time," gasped Drew. "I'd figured a long time ago that we'd never hear of Abe again." His face darkened with a look which did not augur well for Abe. "The bastard never showed up at our prearranged rendezvous. Kept the loot for himself. So, he's turned it into a successful ranch."

"That sure is the end of clever Mr Abe," snapped Dutch. He glared at Shorty. "Where is he?"

"Ah, well, that would be telling," smiled Shorty.

Dutch's lips tightened as he leaned forward. "You little runt," he growled. "Where? Or else this gun blows you to hell."

Shorty eyed him with cold amusement. "That wouldn't be smart. You'd lose the information doing that. Put your gun away, Dutch. You need it less than you need me right now."

Drew put a restraining hand on Dutch's arm. "He's right, Dutch, so ease off." When the gunman had relaxed and holstered his gun, Drew turned to Shorty. "Right, so what have you in mind?"

Shorty drained his glass. "Another beer and then we'll talk some more."

"Get 'em, Dutch," said Drew.

The thickset man pushed himself to his feet and a few moments later slopped beer onto the table as he set three glasses down.

"Right, we're listening," prompted Drew.

Shorty took a sip of his beer, wiped his hand across his mouth and said, "Well, I figure it like this. If Abe Reynolds had met you after the raid, the cash would have been split three ways." He paused and glanced at the two men for confirmation of his supposition. They nodded, and Shorty continued. "I also figure that when you catch up with Abe you'll be mighty sore, in fact I would say his days are numbered."

"Too right they are," snarled Dutch. "I'll blast that hombre so full of lead he'll be ready weighted for the river."

"So, you see, if you cut me in for Abe's share, you'll be no worse off than if he'd met you and you'd split three ways," Shorty pointed out with a smile of satisfaction.

"Why, you pint-sized . . . " Dutch spluttered, his face reddening with astonishment at Shorty's audacity. "A hundred thousand just for information!"

"Ah, but what information," grinned Shorty, raising his eyebrows. "Without it you stay as you are. With it you're richer by a hundred thousand each."

Dutch glared at Shorty and the small man knew that once he had parted with the information he would be a dead man. He'd have to bluff his way into a safe position.

He looked hard at Dutch, his eyes

steeled against the threat. "And don't get ideas about getting rid of me once you have the information you want. I've covered that eventuality. You see, once you have the information, you're going to have to plan your moves."

"We just walk right in on Abe and blast him," snapped Dutch.

Shorty glanced at Drew. "You're going to have to take him in hand, Drew, or else he's going to mess things up again, just as he did at Billings."

Dutch's lips tightened at Shorty's insinuation.

"Cool it, Dutch," hissed Drew. "We want this cash and with the least trouble possible."

"Like I said," went on Shorty, "don't git ideas about me once you have the information. I've left written notes at the bank with instructions to be opened if I meet a violent death — these notes reveal who the rancher is. The authorities will move on him so fast you'll not have time to sort things out." Shorty knew his lies were only a weak protection for his life, but he figured the two outlaws wouldn't examine his words carefully; their minds would be too obsessed with getting their hands on the cash.

"So what's the next move?" pressed Drew.

"We leave tomorrow," said Shorty. "My boss needs two more riders, ready to use guns to implement his plans if necessary. I said I knew two such, didn't mention any names."

"You took a chance on finding me still here," said Drew.

"Sure," agreed Shorty. "And I didn't know Dutch would be here, but thought you might know his whereabouts."

"And it gave you the chance of making some cash," Drew nodded thoughtfully. "Smart thinking. But what if we say we don't want this job and we tail you when you leave . . ."

Shorty interrupted with a sharp laugh of derision. "I'd lose you. Been used to shaking off tails. Like I said, I've ridden the wrong side of the law on occasions, but I've never been caught. And there are a few individuals, who I've given the slip, would like to get their hands on Shorty Wells."

"You've got it all thought out, Shorty," smiled Drew. "So we ain't got anything to do but play along." He glanced at Dutch who nodded his approval.

"Fine," grinned Shorty. "A hundred thousand for me when you get your hands on the cash. But if Abe bought his ranch with it you're going to have to get your hands on that. Now that might work very well."

"You got more in mind?" queried Drew, a note of suspicion creeping in.

Shorty leaned forward. "My boss is interested in the ranch and that's why he wants a couple of extra troubleshooters so's he can use persuasive muscle if necessary."

"But that means we'll be working against ourselves," snapped Dutch. "Hi, what you up to?"

"I ain't up to anything," rapped

Shorty. "Don't you see, if you have to get the ranch off Abe instead of cash, or if you can force him to sell, you've got a ready market — my boss. And you can be on the inside knowing all the moves and can work them to your advantage."

Drew laughed. "You cunning bastard."

"It's up here you want it," smiled Shorty, tapping his forehead. "We ride first thing in the morning."

The following morning three riders left Boulder and headed north.

3

"HELL," snapped Dutch. "How much further? We've been riding four days . . ."

"This is it," cut in Shorty.

The three riders were approaching Two Rivers in the late afternoon.

"Why the hell didn't you say?" growled Dutch irritably. "Thought you were pulling in for another night's stop."

"So this is where Abe finished up?" mused Drew. "No wonder we never found him. He sure moved well away from our usual haunts, to territory we never rode."

"Smart guy," commented Shorty. "You've been riding across his land for the past five hours."

"Have we now?" grinned Dutch, his irritation gone with the thought that this lush grassland could be theirs before very long.

"One last reminder," warned Shorty. "Keep a low profile until you've sized up the situation. Don't forget you're riding for my boss, Mel Clancy. Don't get the wrong side of him."

"Sure, sure," said Drew.

The three horsemen rode along the main street of Two Rivers at a walking pace. They attracted only the odd casual glance with only four people acknowledging Shorty.

Drew studied the town. It was moving with the late afternoon trade. Two wagons, drawn up outside the store, were being loaded by two men bustling with haste. Four ladies emerged from the shop marked Helen's Emporium, schoolkids played tag as they raced from the schoolhouse, two frock-coated gentlemen paused at the entrance to the bank and finished their conversation before they entered the building. Three cowboys lounged in chairs outside the hotel from which two finely dressed ladies emerged. A man led two saddled horses from the livery stable and handed them over to two cowboys, who climbed into saddles and headed out of town by the north road. Next to the livery stable the blacksmith was shoeing a horse while on the opposite side of the street people were gathering outside the stage office in anticipation of meeting friends off the stagecoach due in ten minutes. The door of the sheriff's office opened and a man of medium build stepped on to the sidewalk. He paused as he crammed his stetson on his head. He glanced up the street, his keen, alert eyes taking in the familiar scene, automatically noting anything unusual, out of place. All he saw today were two strangers riding with Shorty Wells, Mel Clancey's troubleshooter.

Drew and Dutch stiffened at the sight of the lawman. They felt his eyes size them up. They tensed, ready for trouble, a natural reaction to seeing a man with a star pinned to his shirt. The sheriff started along the sidewalk, his attention no longer upon them. Drew and Dutch relaxed.

The sound of a piano drifted over the batwings of the gaudily painted saloon with large letters spread across its entire front, announcing that this was The Gilded Cage. As he turned his horse towards the rail and brought it to a halt, Shorty glanced at his two companions. "We'll report to the boss, then you can see to your horses."

Drew and Dutch nodded, swung from their saddles and hitched their horses to the rail. They followed Shorty up the three steps on to the sidewalk and through the swinging batwings. They found themselves in a large room with a stairway, splitting in two to come together at a balcony which ran the full width of the building and gave access to several rooms. The area to the right of the batwings was occupied by gambling tables which were in full session. At the opposite side of the room was the bar, a large ornate mahogany counter, which was matched by the shelving, to the same height, along the wall behind the bar. Above the shelving, running its full length, was a huge mirror. The centre of the floor was taken up with the tables, most of which were occupied by townsfolk and cowboys trying to slake their thirst.

Shorty crossed the room towards a door to the left of the stairs, acknowledging greetings from the three barmen trying to satisfy the demands of the customers.

Drew and Dutch followed Shorty through into a corridor. Shorty stopped at the first door on the right and knocked. At the call of 'Come in', he opened the door and stepped into the elegantly furnished room. Four large leather easy-chairs were arced around an elaborate fireplace. The wooden floor was scattered with rugs and skins. A small table with bottles and glasses stood between the fireplace and a window which looked out on to a high, fenced courtyard. A large table stood against the wall opposite the fireplace with three pictures of Western scenes hanging at eye level. At the far end of the room three high-backed chairs stood in front of a large desk behind which Mel Clancey was signing some papers.

Mel glanced up when the door opened. "Ah, Shorty, glad to see you back," he greeted with a smile as he leaned back in his chair.

"Glad to be back, Mr Clancey," returned Shorty as he started across the room. "Brought the two fellas I told you about." He half-turned as Drew and Dutch strode across the room. "This here's Drew Rogers and Dutch Lowry," he said using the surnames they had agreed upon rather than reveal their true identity.

Mel rose from his chair and came from behind his desk. "Glad to know you," he smiled as he shook hands with both men. He indicated the chairs and the three men sat down as Mel resumed his chair behind the desk. "Shorty will have told you I was looking for a couple of men to ride for me, do what's necessary and ask no questions." He glanced at each of the newcomers in turn.

They nodded. "You can count on us Mr Clancey," said Drew, speaking for both of them.

Mel had been studying the two men. In the tall, wiry Drew he saw a laid-off approach which was deceiving. The eyes were alert, missing nothing, the fingers, long and slender, could be handy with the Colt which hung just right for a quick draw. The stockier, Dutch, seemed to wear a look which spoke of suspicion and ready antagonism. He was a man who would have to be held on a rein or he could stir up trouble when it wasn't wanted.

"Good. Ultimately you're answerable to me but I work through Shorty so you take my orders from him and any others that he sees are necessary when on a job."

Mel's voice was level but incisive, leaving the two men in no doubt that he would stand no nonsense. They had noted the pearl-handled Colt revealed momentarily when he had come to greet them, before his fawn frock-coat covered it. They guessed it wasn't there for show and that the man would not hesitate to use it if the circumstances arose. Until that time it carried a measure of authority. They saw a sharp-featured man, a tight mouth, a determined chin. He was not a man to meddle with, a man used to getting not only his own way but also exactly what he wanted.

"I have big plans for this town," he said. "It's expanding rapidly. Its position, in relation to the river junction and the fords, makes it an ideal site. I have the money to invest, but it's got to be the right places. You help me achieve what I want and I'll be generous. No mistake about that. But cross me, put one foot wrong and — " Mel left the threat unsaid but his action of drawing his forefinger across his throat left no doubt in the minds of his hirelings what would happen. He looked at Shorty. "Two rooms next to yours, see they have what they want."

Shorty nodded and stood up. Drew and Dutch followed suit. When they left the room, Shorty led them to a back door from which he crossed a space to a hut which contained five rooms. "This here's mine," he said, indicating the first door, "you take the next two."

"Who has the others?" queried Dutch.

"One's used by a fella name of Brent Morrison. He doesn't use it all the time and he keeps a very low profile as regards his relationship with Mel. He's got to. You'll be meeting him but around here you ignore him."

"Why?" asked Dutch.

"Don't ask too many questions," replied Shorty. "You can't always have answers." He looked hard at Dutch, making sure he had taken in his meaning.

Dutch grunted.

"Right," went on Shorty. "You saw the livery stable, use it if you want. Clancey has a stable behind this hut if you want to use it, but you'll have to see to your horses yourselves. I use the livery and if I'm going to be around here any length of time I put my horse in the stable rather than leave it in the sun outside the saloon."

"Seems like a good idea," agreed Drew. "We'll do the same."

"One thing I haven't asked you, and Mel will expect I have, I didn't bother because of the bigger stake, but I presume you can handle cattle?" Shorty glanced quickly from one man to the other, trying to get some reaction which they might try to cover.

Drew gave a laconic smile. "Nothing I ain't done. I punched cattle for a few years in northern Montana."

Dutch scowled. "Hell, I thought we were on to bigger things. Didn't expect to be nursemaid to damned cattle."

"I gather you don't like 'em," said Shorty, irritated by Dutch's attitude.

"Don't have to like 'em to manage 'em," muttered Dutch. "I've branded with the best."

"Good," commented a relieved Shorty. "Handling cattle will be only part of the job. Now, one more thing; Abe Reynolds. He's known around here as Doug Walters. For the time being, until you get settled in this job for Mr Clancey you keep a low profile as far as Walters is concerned. If you see him on the street get out of sight. If he comes in the saloon, beat it. You always use the table in the alcove under the stairs. It's next to the door leading to the corridor and through the back door. It gives you a clear view of the batwings without being seen."

"Hell, why can't we go and take him straight away, get our money and then get to hell out of this place?" asked Dutch.

"Questions, questions," rattled Shorty. "I said you can't always have answers but I'll give you one this time. If Reynolds, Walters, used the money from Billings to buy the Circle C then you have to get the Circle C in order to get your cash. Right?" Dutch nodded. "So, if my theories about Clancey's game are correct he wants that land and he'll probably pay over the odds to get it."

"So we don't move on Reynolds until we know what Clancey is up to and when we do we might see the price of the land rocketing."

"Exactly," replied Shorty.

4

CAP MILLET strode onto the veranda of the single-storeyed ranchhouse from which he ran the Flying X ranch eight miles west of Georgetown.

Life was good. His herds were big, with strong cattle. He had a good crew who respected a boss who could and would work alongside them and match them man for man. He had every faith in his foreman, the powerfully built, tough Will Oliver, who had a heart of gold. The men knew a little of Cap's story, knew how he had got his nickname from his rank during the war between the States. They knew how he returned home to find his wife raped and murdered and how he had hunted the killers until he had wreaked a terrible vengeance. They had heard stories of how he had helped clean up Pine Bluffs and there had married his present wife, Laura, after which he had taken to ranching and had built up the Flying X.

Cap stood against the rail and gazed through the early evening light to the far distant mountains, a backcloth to the rolling, luscious prairie grass. He drew deeply on the cool, sweet air, filling his lungs. He let the air out slowly, contentedly. Here was peace and he wanted nothing more than to go on sharing it with Laura. He thanked God for his good fortune in finding love which was returned in full measure, after the desolation of losing his first wife.

"Evening moments, love?" Laura, who had followed him quietly from the house, slipped her arm through his. She knew how Cap loved this time of day just before they had their evening meal, when, with the day's work done, a deeper peace seemed to settle over the land.

"Aye, lass. There's beauty out there

and the change of light alters it every time you look," said Cap quietly as if he was afraid of breaking the tranquillity.

Laura smiled. There were those who would have read Cap's feelings as sentimental weakness, but they would have been wrong. She knew this tall, lean man beside her could be tough, tougher than the next. Galvanized into action he was quick and practice had made him fast with a gun. It was a practice which had grown out of the war and during his terrible mission of revenge. Marks still remained of that time and there were still times when his eyes bore a sadness. Those were times when Laura did not intrude. She knew they did not lessen his love for her.

A gentle movement of air flicked them with a gentle caress. It reminded Laura of the first time they had come to this spot, how it seemed a welcoming touch, telling them they would be happy here. She brushed back the wisps of dark hair which had been disturbed. The movement caught Cap's attention. He glanced at her, admiring the smoothness of her skin and the sparkle in her blue eyes. She too loved this country, vast and sprawling, but good, good to those who loved it. She had a spirited boldness about her which was ever ready to meet a challenge, but she was also gentle and understanding, able to offer advice and make decisions whenever asked but always willing to accept Cap's judgement if they differed.

"Ready to eat?" she asked after a few minutes of shared silence.

Cap nodded, slipped his arm round his wife's waist and started to turn towards the door. His movement was arrested by the sight of a lone rider topping the rise to the north-west of the house.

"What is it?" asked Laura as her husband stopped. She glanced up at him and then followed the shafting of his gaze. "Stranger?" she added, when she saw the object of Cap's attention.

"Don't recognize his sit," replied

Cap, endeavouring to identify him by the way the man rode.

The rider put his horse down the slope, keeping to the same pace, showing no desire to hurry. As he drew nearer, Cap could see the reason why. Both man and his horse looked weary, as if the ride had been long, maybe even hastened until now. Trail dust covered both man and horse.

Cap and Laura waited and watched. When the rider realized there was someone on the veranda, he straightened in the saddle, and tightened his hold on the reins just sufficient to make the ride appear purposeful. The horse responded to his touch and both man and animal looked more resolute.

Cap saw a man whom he judged to be in his mid-twenties, tall, lean, straight-limbed, a man used to a horse. His face was sun and wind burned, indicating a life spent mostly in the open. There was a touch of boldness in his features and, close to, Cap saw an eager brightness in his eyes which, no doubt, had been rekindled after a wearying ride had taken some of the sparkle from them. The man looked as though he was glad to be here, as if he had reached the end of his ride. Cap was curious.

The man pulled his horse to a halt in front of Cap and Laura. He touched the brim of the stained stetson. "Ma'am." The greeting was friendly, respectable and his deep brown eyes smiled at Laura. They moved to Cap. "Sir, do I meet Cap Millet and his wife?"

"You do," returned Cap surprised that this stranger knew them by name. "I'm Cap and this is my wife, Laura."

The man nodded again, then swung from the saddle. The movement was smooth, flowing. He came up the steps, hand extended to Cap. "I'm Matt Sloane," he offered.

Cap took his hand and felt a strong, firm grip. Matt turned to Laura. "I'm sorry to intrude on you, ma'am, but I've had a hard ride with a message from Dorothy Walters."

"Dorothy?" gasped Laura. She glanced at Cap. "We haven't heard of her for over two years."

"Is she all right?" asked Cap.

"She was when I left two days ago. It's her husband, Doug, he's disappeared."

"Disappeared?" Cap frowned. He felt the announcement meant trouble. "No word?"

"None," replied Matt. "Rode out one day to check on some cattle, never came back. We, I work for Doug, we could find no trace of him. Just seemed as if he'd vanished off the face of the earth."

Cap knew Doug as a careful man, well able to take care of himself, yet he would not want to cause Dorothy any anxiety by deliberately staying away.

Cap had first met Dorothy in Pine Bluffs where she was a close friend of Laura's. She had been particularly helpful and loving to Laura when Laura had lost her mother when she was thirteen. Dorothy was five years older than Laura and had married Doug Walters shortly before Cap had arrived in Pine Bluffs. They had left to take up ranching near Two Rivers but in the short time he had known Doug, Cap had liked what he saw. Now they were both successful ranchers. Though news of each other had been sparse over the years they had kept in touch and now it perturbed Cap to think that Dorothy and Doug were in trouble.

"Dorothy, er . . . " Matt faltered then went on, "Mrs Walters sent this note. It may explain more." He handed an envelope to Laura.

Laura, trouble marking her face, took the envelope and slit it open quickly. She extracted a sheet of paper and unfolded it. She read the words quickly and seeing that it contained nothing of a personal nature she read it out.

Dear Laura,
 Please, please help me. Doug has disappeared. I am worried to death.

I don't know where to turn. Matt, who will bring this note, and the rest of the men have done all they could but have found no trace of him. I fear he may have been abducted. Please help.

Love,
Dorothy

Laura looked at her husband with tear-filled eyes. "Oh, Cap, what can we do?"

"We must go to her," replied Cap, a determined light in his eyes.

"Now?"

"First thing in the morning. Matt needs a good night's rest and I want to hear more. From the tone of that note, there's more behind this than first appears." He took the letter from Laura and glanced at it. '*I fear he may have been abducted.*' He looked at Matt. "What's been going on? What does Dorothy mean by that?" Cap did not give Matt time to answer. "We were going to eat, you can join us and tell us what you know. I'll get your horse seen to. You wash up, Laura will show you where."

Laura read the signs. Cap had taken charge and that was the way it would be until he had got to the bottom of the trouble. She indicated to Matt to follow her to the house.

Cap strode from the veranda and hurried to the bunkhouse. Some of the hands were lying on their bunks enjoying a smoke, others were sitting round the table in the centre of the room yarning, while four were getting spruced up for a night in the town. They all looked to the door when it opened.

"Will, stranger name of Matt Sloane's just ridden in. He's staying the night in the ranchhouse. He's had a long hard ride. Have his horse seen to."

"Right, boss," Will Oliver, foreman of the Flying X was on his feet. He was a tall man, broad-shouldered, tough, reliable, one who would stand no nonsense, yet fair in his dealings with his crew, and he had their respect and understanding. When Cap had come to Georgetown, Will had been drifting, having left a foreman's job in Montana. He had liked Cap. Both men had hit it off right from the start and their understanding had a great deal to do with the success of Flying X.

"He'll be leaving in the morning and Laura and I will be riding with him. So have horses ready for a two days' ride." Cap started to turn for the door. "Don't know how long we'll be away, so you're in charge."

Will nodded and glanced over his shoulder. "Shorty, get that hoss."

The cowboy scurried from the room and headed for the ranchhouse.

Will followed Cap outside. "Trouble, Cap?" Out of earshot of the men, Will used the familiar address, gleaned from Cap's days in the Union Army during the war. Will knew the signs in his boss.

Cap shrugged. "Don't really know. Cry for help from an old friend of

Laura's down in Two Rivers. Gotta go."

"Want any help along?" asked Will.

"No. That could be a waste of time. Besides, from what this hombre says, I figure there's a decent crew at the Circle C."

"Doug Walter's place?" Will's remark came as something of a surprise to Cap.

"Yes. Know it?"

"Rode for him for about a year, then felt like drifting, so left."

"Any reason why Doug should disappear?" pressed Cap.

Will's lips tightened thoughtfully for a second then shook his head. "Wasn't there long and everything seemed all right when I left."

"You looked thoughtful for a moment, Will. Something trouble you?" Cap had seized on that slight hesitation before Will had answered him.

"Well, nothing specific. Just, I didn't like Doug's foreman. He was a reason why I left. Didn't like his methods and he was too cocky."

"Name?" asked Cap.

"Brent Morrison."

Cap nodded. "Anything else to tell me?"

Will shook his head. "Like I said, I wasn't there long. But watch out for Morrison. He's rough, tough, handy with his gun and a knife, and he'll use his fists."

"Thanks, Will." Cap tapped his foreman appreciatively on his arm. "Good-night."

Cap hurried away.

"Night, boss," Will called after him.

5

WHEN Cap reached the ranch-house, Laura was busy in the kitchen.

"Oh, Cap, do you think Doug will be all right?" she asked anxiously.

"I hope so, love," he replied, putting a comforting arm round her shoulders. "Matt?" he asked.

"I've put him in the west bedroom," replied Laura. "Seems likeable."

They heard a movement in the corridor which led to the three bedrooms.

"Go see him, Cap. I'll have the food out in a minute."

"Nice place you've got here Mister Millet," observed Matt as the two men entered the main room in the house.

The room was large, with skin rugs scattered across the wooden floor. Three big settees and four armchairs did not overwhelm the room, at one end of which was a dining-table with six chairs round it.

"Hi, if we're riding the trail together leave off the Mister, it's Cap."

A little embarrassed, Matt grinned. "Sure, if that's the way you want it."

"It is. I ain't used to handles like Mister," returned Cap.

While they were speaking, Cap was studying the young cowboy. He had an open face with a ready smile and Cap reckoned he would be loyal to the point of obsession. Matt had changed into a pair of clean jeans and checked shirt. His boots had been cleaned of the dust and now shone as if they had never been marked by a long ride. He was a man who obviously cared about his appearance and respected the fact that Cap and Laura had welcomed him to their home, whereas they could so easily have had him bunk with the hands.

"Come on you two, sit down," called Laura as she came in from the kitchen with a bowl of steaming broth.

The two men crossed the room and Matt accepted the seat indicated by Cap.

Matt relished the broth after two days on hardtack on the trail and was into the main course of beef, potatoes and vegetables before Cap broached the subject of Doug's disappearance.

"Right, Matt, I reckon you've got the edge off your appetite so I figure we can start talking," he said, glancing at Matt as he sliced his meat. "First, what's your position at the Circle C?"

"Top hand."

Cap nodded. "Who's your foreman?"

"Clint Turner."

Cap looked up with surprise, "Thought it was Brent Morrison."

Matt hesitated with a potato half-way to his mouth. He lowered it slowly as he met Cap's gaze. "You testing me out?" There was a slight edge to his voice.

"No, no," Cap hastened to reassure him. "My foreman apparently rode for the Circle C for a year, he just told me."

"And I suppose Brent Morrison was foreman when he was there?" asked Matt.

"Said so," replied Cap.

"Wal, he ain't any longer," said Matt. "Doug sacked him, six months back."

Cap's attention sharpened. Could this have something to do with Doug's disappearance? "Why?"

"He was a bit heavy-handed with the crew, got worse, some hands left. But Brent was good around cattle."

"Tough, handy with a gun, a knife and his fists, so Will tells me."

"Your foreman sure has him sussed out," commented Matt. "But maybe he didn't tell you Brent was a ladies' man — he had the looks and knew it. Figured he was irresistible. Thought the sun just came up to hear him crow. That was his undoing. He made a play for Dorothy. Doug and I walked in when he was mauling her. Doug went for him, didn't give Brent a chance — a right to the stomach followed by a vicious uppercut sent Brent sprawling. Doug went for his gun but Dorothy stopped him."

"Brent retaliate?" asked Cap.

"No, not even a word. He hightailed it out of there and a few minutes later was riding away from the Circle C with Doug threatening to kill him if he saw him near the ranch again."

"Had he pestered Dorothy before?" asked Laura tentatively, as if she was afraid the answer might be yes.

"Don't know, ma'am, I figure not, the way Dorothy was reacting when we walked in. She sure was making a struggle. She said he'd come looking for Doug, started sweet-talking her and using his hands."

Laura looked relieved. She had figured that Dorothy wouldn't have given the foreman any encouragement and she was pleased to have confirmation.

"Could this have anything to do with Doug's disappearance?" asked Cap.

Matt took some vegetables while looking thoughtful, weighing up the answer he should

"Revenge, you mean?" Cap nodded. "Not sure," Matt went on. "Could be. Brent's the type of man who could bear a grudge and he sure wouldn't like getting whipped the way he was, especially in front of a lady."

Matt respected the silence which Cap seemed to want to sort out the information he had been given. The meal continued quietly until Cap laid down his knife and fork.

"Anything else to tell me?" he asked.

"Let Matt finish his meal first," admonished Laura, though she was as eager as her husband for more information.

"Sorry, Matt. I'm spoiling your meal," Cap apologized.

"That's all right," replied Matt. He quickly finished his meat and the remaining potatoes. As Laura was clearing the plates away, Matt looked at Cap. "Yes, there is something else.

Doug's been losing cattle over the past year."

"Rustling?" asked Cap, alert to the possible implications.

"At first we thought they had strayed but when we missed them more regularly we figured they were being rustled. Never more than ten at a time and more often less than that."

"That few?" remarked Cap with surprise. "Somebody setting up a herd."

"We've searched, we've set traps for the rustlers, but nothing worked and we never found any trace of the cattle."

"You said this has been going on over the past year?" Matt nodded his confirmation. "Then it started before Brent Morrison was sacked."

"Sure," agreed Matt. "You were thinking there might be some connection. Rustling as part of the revenge."

"Could have been."

"Unlikely. Brent was keen to catch the rustlers."

Cap made no comment. He kept his thoughts to himself. Had Brent Morrison been trying to set up a herd for himself even before he had left the Circle C?

"In her note, Dorothy says she fears Doug may have been abducted. What's behind that?" asked Cap.

"Don't know," returned Matt with a puzzled shake of his head. "Unless she thinks Brent may have done so."

Cap looked thoughtful. "Could be," he said, but he sounded doubtful.

"You think there might be some other reason for Dorothy to say that?" said Matt.

"Don't know," replied Cap. "She doesn't mention Brent in her letter so there could be something else that you don't know about."

Matt nodded his understanding. "Well, there's only one person who can tell us that — Dorothy, so the sooner we reach the Circle C the better."

Laura came back with plates and a

large apple pie, the crust of which was golden brown.

"That looks mighty good, ma'am," said Matt, eyeing the pie with anticipatory pleasure.

Laura smiled at his enthusiasm. "I hope it tastes as good."

As Laura cut the pie, Cap glanced at Matt. "You're more than concerned about Doug's disappearance, aren't you?" he commented.

"I am. It's hit Dorothy hard. Mr and Mrs Walters were very kind to me when I was looking for a job. I was seventeen at the time. Had no folks of my own. Only child. Ma and pa had been killed during a bank hold-up in Billings where we lived — Fenton gang, got away with a lot of money. I drifted and was getting desperate when I asked for a job at the Circle C. Willing to do anything. Doug and Dorothy seemed to take a liking to me. Treated me like I was their own son. Couldn't figure why they took to a brat like me."

"You play yourself down, Matt,"

put in Laura. "Look at you, a fine upstanding young fella."

Matt grinned. "You should have seen me at seventeen. I was a precocious brat all right, with a chip on my shoulder. The world had taken my ma and pa and it owed me. But Dorothy and Doug treated me right, maybe it was because they had no family of their own. So you see, Cap, I am concerned. Doug taught me all he could about cattle and horses and I learn fast, and although I say it myself, I'm good."

"Guess you must be if you're top-hand," Cap smiled at the young man's confidence. "Get on well with the rest of the outfit?"

"Sure."

"They don't resent any special treatment 'cos Doug took to you?"

"Special treatment?" Matt laughed. "When it came to working I was just one of the crew as far as Doug was concerned."

"Pleased to know it," Cap approved. "How about Brent Morrison? How did he like Doug's concern for you?"

"Made it rough at times, but I took it. He respected me for it. Doug wanted to intervene but I told him I'd ride out if he did and I figure he respected me for it too."

"Your ma and pa?" asked Laura.

"Kept a store in Billings," said Matt. A sadness touched his eyes. "They'd gone to the bank and were coming out when the Fenton gang hit it. The gang were rumbled and there was a lot of gunfire. Ma and pa were in the way as the gang broke out — they . . ." Matt's voice faltered as he recalled the fatal day.

"I'm sorry, Matt," said Laura with concern as she laid a comforting hand on Matt's arm. "Shouldn't have asked."

Matt looked sharply. "That's all right ma'am." A gleam came to his eyes. "I swore I'd get them. I really did — you know, a kid's cry in the wilderness."

"And now?" prompted Cap. "How do you feel now?"

Matt pursed his lips. "It's something I've thought about. I've been shown kindness; I've got a new life; why should I bear a grudge? What happened, happened. I can't change that. But you know, if I came face to face with one of the gang I reckon I'd be back in Billings seeing my ma and pa shot down and I figure there'd be no stopping me taking revenge."

"Understandable," commented Cap quietly. "Did you see the gang in Billings? You'd know them?"

Matt's lips tightened. He shook his head. "I was the other side of town. Wouldn't know them if I passed them in the street."

"Any of the gang get caught?" asked Laura.

"Not one," said Matt. "Two were killed during the raid, one of them was the leader Gil Fenton. The other three went to ground and have never been heard of since. No need with the haul they got. Three hundred thousand dollars."

Cap let out a low whistle. "As much as that?" He gave a half laugh. "Then I figure you'll never have a run-in with any of them. They'll be scattered and living under assumed names. And you not able to recognize them."

Cap held his plate for more pie. "Tell me, Matt, what's the sheriff of Two Rivers done about Doug's disappeareance?"

"Aw, him." There was a dismissive note of contempt in Matt's voice. "He's gone through the motions, done some questioning, ridden with us, tried to figure if there's any connection between rustling and Doug's disappearance, but didn't do any real digging. Seemed to take it that Doug was dead. But then maybe that was just a blind. You see, Mel Clancey, big shot in Two Rivers, has him in his pocket."

Cap glanced sharply at Matt. "You hinting that this here Clancey could be . . ."

"Hold on," Matt interrupted. "I ain't accusing anybody. Can't. But Clancey runs the sheriff, so if he has anything to do with Doug's disappearance, though I can't see why he would be involved, he could get the sheriff to play down his investigations."

Cap nodded thoughtfully. "So it would be wise for me not to approach the sheriff, not involve him, play a lone hand instead?"

"Right," agreed Matt. "That way nothing from you will get back to Clancey."

"Good, we'll play it that way." Cap put the final seal on his approach to the problem.

6

WILL OLIVER had the three horses ready by eight the next morning. When he and two of the other hands brought them to the ranchhouse, Cap introduced Matt to them.

"Matt tells me Brent Morrison no longer rides with the Circle C," said Cap.

"It'll be a better outfit without him," commented Will.

"Been gone six months," said Matt.

"How long you been riding with them?" asked Will.

"Five years," replied Matt.

"I left seven years ago 'cos of Brent Morrison," said Will, steadying Laura's horse as she slung the saddle-bags across its back and tied her bedroll behind the saddle. "I was drifting when I met the boss." He nodded in Cap's direction. "Best thing that happened to me. Remember me to Walters when you see him."

"Sure will," said Matt. He swung into the saddle and held the animal under control.

Cap gave some last-minute instructions to Will and helped Laura to mount her horse. She was neatly but practically dressed in a split riding-skirt and an open-necked blouse with a bandana tied neatly at her throat. She wore calf-length riding-boots, matched by black gloves and a black, low-crowned sombrero. She settled herself in the saddle and handled her horse skilfully as she turned it away from the house.

Cap climbed into the saddle, turned his horse and with a raised hand to bid goodbye, tapped the horse into a trot. Laura and Matt followed suit and the trio headed away from the Flying X.

They kept their mounts to a pace which conserved their energy and was not tiring upon themselves. They had a long ride ahead with two nights respite from their saddle.

They moved into the lush grassland of the foothills of the mountains shortly after they broke camp following their second night's stop.

"Good cattle country," commented Cap.

"Aye, it is," agreed Matt. "We're on Circle C range now. Just before noon we'll hit the depression which runs all the way up to the ranchhouse."

The sun was high when they rounded a hillside in the rolling grassland and moved into a dip which was lined on two sides by low, rounded hills.

At the far end of this shallow valley they could see a group of buildings set against a backcloth of higher ground where the hillsides which formed the hollow swung to meet each other.

"Lovely setting," commented Laura, as, with the house in sight, eagerness to meet her old friend gripped her.

"And sheltered on three sides," said

Matt. "Ideal position. Doug chose well."

"Trail from Two Rivers?" asked Cap.

"Lies about a mile over the hill at the back of the house," explained Matt. "Runs between Two Rivers and Pincher Creek. Two Rivers ain't all that big, but it's bigger than Pincher Creek and is nearer. 'Bout ten miles away, Pincher's 'bout twenty-five."

They tapped their horses into a trot and Cap studied the buildings on the ride in. As he expected they were well maintained. The ranchhouse, with its long front veranda, was L-shaped. The bunkhouse stood about two hundred yards to the right with the stables beyond that. Four corrals broke up some of the ground to their right. In one of them four cowboys were breaking in a horse which Cap reckoned had come from several occupying a neighbouring corral.

"You run horses as well as cattle," observed Cap, with a glance at Matt.

"There's plenty running wild in the hills west of here," explained Matt. "Doug has a nice thing going, breaking 'em in and selling 'em to the Army."

Cap pursed his lips and nodded. As far as he could see there was nothing in that which could cause Doug trouble unless he had discovered someone else trying to get in on the trade.

They were still about a quarter of a mile from the house when they saw someone come onto the veranda.

"Dorothy!" exclaimed Laura and immediately sent her horse into a fast run.

She was swinging out of the saddle before her mount had come to a halt. Pleasure danced in her eyes as she held out her arms to Dorothy who was running to meet her. The two friends hugged each other tightly.

"Oh, Laura, I'm so glad you've come," gasped Dorothy. The words choked in her throat and tears filled her eyes.

"It's good to be with you," returned

Laura, giving her friend an extra-tight hug, imparting comfort and reassurance. "Everything's going to be all right."

"Oh I hope so," cried Dorothy. "I'm worried stiff about Doug. I didn't know what to do."

Laura eased her away to give her a confidence-raising look. "You did right to send for us. Cap will find Doug."

Dorothy turned and held out her hand to Cap who was climbing from the saddle. Cap took her hand with a firm but gentle touch, and kissed her lightly on the cheek.

"Thanks for coming, Cap." Dorothy suppressed the tears of relief, but Cap sensed her feelings at having someone, other than the Circle C hands, to turn to.

"That's what friends are for," he replied. "I only hope I can do something."

"It's a great comfort to have you here," said Dorothy. "Now, come on in, you must be tired after your ride, and hungry." She turned to Matt. "Thanks for bringing them, Matt."

He nodded and asked, "No news since I left?"

"None," replied Dorothy sadly.

Matt's lips tightened in exasperation. "I'm sure everything will turn out right, now Cap's here. I'll see the horses are taken care of." He turned his horse and started towards the bunkhouse.

"Thanks, Matt," called Cap.

Matt raised his hand in acknowledgement.

"Likeable chap," commented Cap as Dorothy took them to the house.

"Yes," replied Dorothy. "Glad you got on well with him, thought you would."

As she led the way into the single-storeyed house, Cap was able to study her. He saw a friend who appeared to have aged since they last saw each other seven years ago, but figured some of the appearance was caused by the worry and anxiety of the past few weeks. Behind the trouble-lines he could still see the serenity of a woman who had come to terms with the life of a rancher's wife. He remembered the tranquil light which always seemed to shine from the pale blue eyes, and the adoration which emanated from her love for Doug. Her deep black hair which had always been neatly drawn back to a bun in the nape of her neck, now had a few loose wisps straggling to her shoulders. With the object of her love gone she had not bothered to put the final touches to her appearance, as was also evidenced by her gingham dress which was showing signs of having been worn longer than normal.

There were two doors on each side of the square entrance. The first one on the left was open and revealed a long room, part of which held some easy-chairs while the far end was occupied by a table for dining. From the noise which came from the second door on the left Laura and Cap knew it was the kitchen.

"Chang's a bit noisy when he's getting a meal ready," explained Dorothy.

"You've a Chinese cook?" exclaimed Laura with some surprise.

"Yes. Had him two years. He's excellent," replied Dorothy.

"Any particular reason for hiring a Chinaman?" asked Cap, his mind already looking at possibilities for Doug's disappearance.

"No. Doug was looking to ease my work. Chang had tried to escape poverty in China by coming here with the gangs hired to construct the railroads. It was rough in the mountains. They were mistreated so he left them, escaped, came further east. He turned up in Two Rivers. First Chinaman seen there. He was being given a hard time until Doug hired him. I'd better tell him there'll be two more. Won't be a moment. Wait in here." Dorothy opened the first door on the right before going to the kitchen.

Laura and Cap found themselves in a large room, comfortably furnished with settee and easy-chairs, with a desk at the far end.

"They've a nice set-up here," remarked Laura.

"Sure have. Hope nothing's happened to Doug to upset it," said Cap.

"Any ideas?" asked Laura, crossing to a window from which she saw two cowboys leading their horses away. She glanced over her shoulder to see Cap shrug his shoulders, but before he could answer her the door opened and Dorothy joined them.

"I'll show you your room, you can freshen up. There'll be some coffee ready and then I'm anxious to talk."

Dorothy led the way through the entrance hall to the second door on the left. This led into a passage which ran along the back of the house and turned into the projection situated at right angles to the main part of the building. Here were three bedrooms, the third one of which was for Laura and Cap, the first being used by Dorothy and Doug.

Once they had washed off the dust of the ride and changed into fresh clothes, Laura and Cap joined Dorothy in the main room.

Before they were seated, Chang entered the room with a tray containing three cups, a steaming jug of coffee and a plate with some biscuits.

When Dorothy made the introductions, Chang smiled and bowed politely before hurrying off to his kitchen.

The three friends sat down and Dorothy poured the coffee. "I'm so grateful to you for coming," she said as she handed the coffee round. "I've been past myself with worry."

"If you feel like talking then tell me what you know," suggested Cap as he settled back in an easy-chair with his coffee.

Dorothy offered him a biscuit. He bit into it and his eyes widened.

"Mmm, Chang make these?" he asked, savouring the rich, treacle taste.

Dorothy nodded, "Sure."

"If the rest of his cooking's like this then I'm going to be mighty happy," commented Cap. "Better get this recipe, Laura."

Laura smiled and agreed when she tasted her biscuit, but she knew that behind Cap's words was an attempt to put Dorothy at her ease to talk about Doug's disappearance.

"How much did Matt tell you?" asked Dorothy.

"Said Doug rode out to check on some cattle and never came back," replied Cap. "Told me you had cattle rustled over the past year, in small numbers. Also that six months ago Doug sacked your foreman, Brent Morrison, after he caught him make a play at you."

Dorothy's cheeks coloured. She nodded. "Unpleasant business," she said. "Couldn't understand Brent. He'd been here a long time. He was a good foreman, knew cattle. Hard working."

"You defending him?" asked Cap sharply.

"Cap!" Laura admonished her husband with the timbre of her crisp intonation.

"I've got to explore every possibility," replied Cap. "I'm sorry, Dorothy."

"It's all right, Cap," returned Dorothy, regaining her composure quickly after the initial shock of Cap's question. "No, I'm not defending him. Just telling you what the man is like. He's tough and for some reason, don't know why, he would suddenly become a bit heavy-handed with the crew. Men would leave. But I figure it was only phases he went through. Doug was successful in calming the men concerned and persuading them to stay."

"Matt told me he's a ladies' man," said Cap. "Had he ever made a play for you before?"

Dorothy blushed. She shook her head. "Never. Oh, he's eyed me up and down and left me in no doubt about his thoughts but he always kept his distance until that day. He came looking for Doug and I was alone in the house. Whether he knew Doug wasn't there I don't know. No doubt Matt told you what happened."

"Yes," Cap nodded. "Could I have some more coffee, please?" He handed his cup to Dorothy, deliberately making a break in his line of questioning to ease the unsavoury incident from her mind.

Dorothy poured the coffee, handed the cup back to Cap and offered him the plate of biscuits.

"Mighty fine these," he said and took two. "Thanks."

"More for Laura?" Dorothy turned to her friend.

"Please," said Laura, extending the time between questions on purpose.

"Right," said Cap when they had all settled down again. "The rustling, tell me about that."

"Started about a year ago. Just a few at a time."

"Had Doug any suspicions about

who might be doing it?"

"When it first started he thought it might be some mavericker starting to build up a herd, but he threw that idea out when it continued."

"On the assumption that a mavericker would get the nucleus and then move out," prompted Cap as Dorothy hesitated.

"Yes," she agreed. "But with the rustling continuing he began to think it might be someone local."

"Did he voice any names?" asked Cap.

Dorothy shrugged her shoulders. "Names get bantered about in conversation — you know how it is."

"Tell me," pressed Cap.

"Well, when Brent left he came under suspicion — doing it for revenge, but Doug wiped that idea out because the rustling had been going on before Brent left."

"Anybody else?"

"Well, you begin to suspect anybody. Mick Owens, for instance. He owns the

Running W, to the south, our nearest neighbour. But Mick's too straight, always been a good friend, there's never been any animosity between us. He runs a tight crew so don't figure any of them would step out of line."

"Other neighbours?"

Dorothy pursed her lips and shook her head.

"No one to the west, too near the mountains. North, they're twenty miles beyond Two Rivers. East, there's two ranches but they are a good fifty miles from us."

"They can ride," Cap pointed out.

"Sure, but if they'd rustled the cattle they'd have been seen or at least tracked down. They'd have had a lot of open country to cross, because the cattle always disappeared from the west range," explained Dorothy. She sipped her coffee.

Cap puckered his lips thoughtfully. "Handy for broken country through the foothills and into the mountains."

"Exactly," agreed Dorothy emphatically.

"And never a trace found?" asked Cap.

"None. The crew, led by Doug, searched but came up with nothing. Whoever was doing it was always careful to hide their tracks. Whenever Doug put a watch on the cattle nothing happened. It was almost as if whoever was behind it knew our moves, but then you can't keep watch on every steer all the time. The herds are big and they roam. Reckon it was always easy for someone to pick off a few."

Cap took a drink and nodded his agreement, but he was interested in the fact that Dorothy seemed to think that their moves were known. He made no comment but locked the information away in his mind.

"Anybody else whom you might suspect?" asked Cap.

"No," replied Dorothy. "But I've had two offers for the ranch since Doug disappeared."

"What!" Cap's surprise showed and

he shot a glance at Laura who was equally taken aback by Dorothy's announcement. Cap leaned forward and put his cup on the low table between himself and Dorothy. "Who?"

"Mick Owens was one," replied Dorothy.

"Interesting," mused Cap.

"The other's more interesting," Dorothy went on. "Surprising. Mel Clancey, owner of The Gilded Cage and a lot of other property in Two Rivers."

Cap raised his eyebrows. "Ranching seems an unlikely interest for a saloon and property owner," he commented. "Has he had any connection with ranching before?"

"Not that I know of," replied Dorothy. "Told me he was just looking to expand his interests around Two Rivers. He oozed charm when he came to see me. Said he regretted approaching this subject at this trying time but he didn't want anyone else to step in if Doug had really gone missing and I was prepared to sell up and leave."

"Did they both offer you a price?" asked Cap.

"Yes," replied Dorothy. Very similar so they had both sized up the value of the property before approaching me. I checked afterwards and neither of them were trying to do me down."

"Can you tell me more about this Clancey fella?" asked Cap.

"He came to Two Rivers shortly after we came here. Of his background I know nothing. Never heard it spoken about. He took over The Gilded Cage, built it up on a good reputation — fair gaming tables, plenty of liquor and good-looking girls. He gradually bought up other property — the hotel, the livery stable, the store. Has a manager run that for him. Opened another saloon, not as opulent as The Gilded Cage, but it offers food for the cowboys. If you want a bit more elegance with your dining you go to his hotel. One could say he's been good for

Two Rivers if you wanted it to grow. Maybe he saw the potential of being near the junction of rivers with their small but important river traffic and also the fact that just downstream of the junction there's a good ford, and both have fords upstream."

"So there's every chance of Two Rivers becoming important?" said Laura.

"Possibly," replied Dorothy. "But we've heard of these towns with potential which hasn't materialized and they've grown no more or contracted into hick towns. I suppose the growth of Two Rivers could depend on whether the railway decide to run a line either to or through here."

"Well, thanks Dorothy," said Cap, "I'm beginning to get a picture. Now tell me about the day Doug disappeared."

"Not a lot to tell," replied Dorothy. She put down her cup and glanced at her hands for a moment. There was sadness in her eyes when she looked at Cap again. The memories of that day haunted her.

"Miss nothing out. An insignificant detail might give us a clue," prompted Cap gently.

"Well, we were up at our usual early time, 6.30. We were having breakfast when Doug told me he was going to check the cattle to the north-west."

"Did he give any particular reason for going there?" interrupted Cap.

"No, but it was the area where most cattle have disappeared."

"Had he any night riders out?"

"Not on this occasion. Things had been quiet for a while — no rustling. Night riding disrupts the day's work so, as things had quietened down, Doug had dispensed with them. But he still kept strict daylight checks. A rider would go out and report back if he figured anything was wrong."

"Did he go alone?" asked Cap.

"Sure, there was no reason why he shouldn't. I mean, we never expected this to happen."

"But supposing the rider came upon someone in the act?"

"If that happened the rider had strict instructions not to tackle the rustlers but to either trail them or get back here as quick as possible."

"So Doug went alone," prompted Cap.

"Yes. I watched him ride off and that's the last I saw of him." The words caught in Dorothy's throat. She swallowed hard and took a grip on her feelings. "I got worried in the late afternoon when Doug hadn't returned. I was worried in case he'd had an accident and was lying out there injured. I got our foreman, Clint Turner, to organize a search party. He figured it was a wise thing to do before it got dark. I rode with them. We found nothing. No sign of Doug, nor his horse. We came back and continued the search throughout the next few days. Still nothing. Then, in desperation, I contacted you."

"Has Doug ever gone off on his own

before, maybe for a few days hunting and fishing up in the mountains?" asked Laura.

Dorothy shook her head. "Not without telling me. And when he has done so he's taken Matt with him."

"Strange you found no trace whatsoever. If he'd had an accident you'd have thought you'd have found his horse," mused Cap.

"There was no sign of it," Dorothy reaffirmed.

"You said in your letter you feared he might have been abducted." Cap watched Dorothy carefully for her reaction. "What did you mean by that?"

Dorothy hesitated. She diverted her gaze from Cap, then said, in a voice that pretended certainty, "Oh, nothing. It was just me, extra worried when I wrote that letter." Dorothy tried to dismiss the matter, but Cap realized that there was something she was reluctant to divulge.

He looked hard at her as she glanced

up to see if her excuse was sufficient. "Dorothy, if I am to help I need to know everything." His voice was firm. "We're friends, you can confide in us."

Dorothy bit her lip and regarded her two friends apprehensively.

"Whatever it is, Dorothy, you know it will go no further." Laura spoke softly, reassuring her friend, encouraging her to speak.

Dorothy dampened her lips, a sign of gaining confidence. She nodded. "You're right. I should tell you." She straightened, stiffening her back, and drew a deep breath. "I fear he may have been kidnapped by the Fenton gang."

The announcement stunned both Cap and Laura. The immediate silence hung heavy with surprise.

"The Fenton gang? Why the Fenton gang?" Cap broke the silence with a gasp. "Nothing's been heard of them since they took 300,000 dollars from the bank in Billings. I should think not, with cash like that in their pockets."

"Doug was one of them!" Dorothy's words, quiet, reluctant to come out penetrated the bemused minds of her listeners.

"What!" Laura and Cap gasped together. They exchanged a quick glance and each knew that Matt's threat against the Fenton gang had sprung to mind.

"But . . . what . . . " Cap foundered.

"It's true," Dorothy began her explanation. "It was a secret between us. Doug's real name is Abe Reynolds. He rode with the Fentons but after the last bank raid, when innocent people got killed, he was sickened. Pursuit was hot after that raid and the gang scattered. Doug had the loot. Sickened as he was, he wanted out so he did a deal with the authorities — return the money, without personal contact, for his freedom. He also stipulated that news of the recovery of the money should be kept quiet. He figured if the gang heard, they'd come gunning for him."

"But didn't he reckon that they'd look for him in order to get their share of the cash?" said Cap.

"Sure, but if they'd known he'd returned it, all that they would be intent on would be to kill him — a bullet in the back would do. Whereas if they didn't know then he had a chance — they'd want him alive. However he hoped they'd never catch up with him. He took on a new identity, a new name. That's when he came to Pine Bluffs. We fell in love."

"Did he not . . . ?" began Laura.

Dorothy gave her a wan smile. "Oh, yes, Doug was straight, he told me. Said he couldn't marry me without me knowing. Said he'd understand if I wanted to call it off. But I was in love with the man I knew, not a member of the Fenton gang. There was no need for anyone else to know. We moved here, settled, you can see the result. We hoped the Fenton gang would never find him. Time went by and it seemed we'd won. We never heard anything of them and they faded from our minds."

"But now you wonder," said Laura.

"Wouldn't you?" answered Dorothy.

"Have you any reason to think that they're around?" asked Cap.

"A month ago, Doug came home from Two Rivers. I could tell something was bothering him, he was on edge. At first he just said he was not feeling well, but I knew otherwise and eventually, after my insistence, he told me that he thought he had seen Dutch Hardy, one of the gang, in Two Rivers."

"Was he certain?" queried Cap.

"No, it was just a glimpse in the distance. Doug tried to pick up the man's movements but he'd disappeared."

"There's been no further contact?" Dorothy shook her head. "None."

"No strangers around the ranch?"

"No."

"A month ago, you said."

"Yes."

"I would have thought that if it was

Dutch Hardy the gang would have made their play before now. But you never know, they may have had their reasons. Do you know the names of the rest of the gang?"

"Gil Fenton, Blackie Fisher, they were killed during the raid, and . . ." Dorothy paused, delving into her memory. "Yes, got it. Drew Kinkaid."

"Anything else?" asked Cap.

Dorothy shook her head. "No, I don't think so."

"Thanks for being so frank," Cap said. "You've been a great help."

Dorothy looked at him pleadingly. "Do you think you can find him?"

"I'll do my best," replied Cap.

"And Doug's past won't matter?" asked Dorothy tentatively.

"The man I know is the man you married, a man who became a successful rancher and one I know as a friend."

7

EARLY the following morning, Cap sought out Clint Turner.

"Cap Millet," he introduced himself to the foreman.

"Glad to know you," returned Clint. "Doug spoke about you. His disappearance sticks in my craw. We all feel so helpless, not finding even a trace." The foreman's face clouded with frustration.

"Let's hope I have better luck," said Cap. "I'm going to start by riding over to see Mike Owens. Like to have Matt show me the way," he requested.

"Sure." Clint turned to a group of cowboys who were heading for the corrals. "Hi, Matt, saddle up and ride with Mr Millet."

Matt raised his hand in acknowledgement. He spoke to one of the men in the group and they both turned in the direction of the stables. "We'll see to your horse," Matt called.

"Thanks," acknowledged Cap. He turned to Clint. "And cut out the Mister," he said with a friendly smile. "It's Cap from now on."

"Sure thing," replied Clint, pleased that things would be kept informal. He worked better that way. "Mick Owens?" He gave a slight shake of his head. "If you don't mind me saying so, I reckon he's clean. Not the type. He's always been a good neighbour."

"Do we ever know anyone really well?" mused Cap, thinking of Doug's real identity.

Clint looked thoughtful. "Well, maybe not, but I'll stake anything that Mick had nothing to do with this."

"You're most likely right," said Cap, "but I've got to look at every angle."

"Sure."

"You probably don't know, but since Doug disappeared Owens has offered to buy Circle C." Cap lowered his voice.

"What!" Clint gasped, and Cap saw genuine surprise on his face, confirming the opinion Cap had formed that Clint was a straight, good working, honest, foreman.

"It's true. Dorothy told me. Keep that strictly to yourself, and I mean yourself." Cap emphasized his words.

"It'll go no further, Cap," Clint assured him emphatically. "Dorothy didn't . . . ?"

Cap shook his head. "No. She's not prepared to consider any offer. She believes Doug will be back."

He saw relief on Clint's face. "Wonder why Owens made that move now?" queried the foreman.

"That's one thing I aim to find out," said Cap.

Matt and the Circle C hand emerged from the stable with the two horses, and led them over to the two men.

"Thanks," said Cap as he took the reins. He swung into the saddle and settled himself as he held his mount steady. "See you later, Clint." Cap sent his horse forward and Matt moved alongside him.

They rode through open country, moving nearer the foothills. They saw herds of prime cattle grazing peacefully on the range with the lush grassland covering the low hills.

Cap questioned Matt about Mick Owens and learned that he was a man who had come young to this country, and had wrestled with it and won, carving out a ranch second to none for more than five hundred miles around.

"His only regret," said Matt, "is that he did not take in more land and build a huge cattle empire."

"Could he be trying to do that now?"

Matt looked at Cap with surprise. "You mean he's behind the rustling, trying to force Doug to sell?"

"And kidnapping a stubborn Doug to . . . " Cap left the suggestion unfinished and added, "All things are possible, such things have happened before."

Matt gave a half a laugh of doubt. "Sure, but Mick and Doug were good friends." He looked thoughtful for a moment and shook his head. "No, no, couldn't be."

"You are most likely right, but I've got to look at all possibilities," Cap pointed out. "Owens got any family?"

"One son, Pete. Father dotes on him. Spoils him but he's brought him up tough. Wants him to be exactly like himself. Pete's a bit of a harum-scarum, wild, gets into all sorts of scrapes, father has to bail him out, smooth things over, you know how it is with a son who wants for nothing. Boy acts tough, and he is, he'll work alongside and as good as any hand but he has a weak spot, maybe inherited from his mother. I'm told she was a nice lady who sadly died when Pete was only ten."

"So Mick's had to be father and mother to Pete," mused Cap. "That don't always work for the good of the child."

"Surely that don't have anything to do with Doug's disappearance?" queried Matt.

"Most likely not, but it gives me a better picture of Mick," replied Cap, easing himself in the saddle. "Let's wait and see."

Ten minutes later, Matt pulled his horse to a halt at the top of a low hill. "The Running W," he said as Cap reined his horse alongside.

Below them, at the foot of a gentle slope, sheltered by the hill, lay a ranchhouse and the usual buildings of bunkhouse, stables and sheds. The whole was neat and tidy, with the fences of the corrals in good shape. Several cowboys were working horses in two of the corrals. There was an air of efficiency in a well-run ranch.

The two men kept their mounts to a walking pace as they approached the ranchhouse. They drew the attention of some of the cowboys who, recognizing Matt, raised their hands in a gesture of greeting.

As they were fastening their horses to the hitching rail in front of the veranda of the house, a big, broadset man threw open the door and hurried out. He pulled up short when he saw the new arrivals. His lips were tight, emphasizing the annoyance which clouded his face. His eyes swept over Cap and settled on Matt. "God give me strength!" The words exploded in short gasps as he raised his eyes heavenwards. "Why can't that son of mine be like you Matt?" He glanced back at Cap. "Sorry, stranger." His tone became more amiable. "You've walked in on a family dispute."

"We all have 'em," replied Cap casually.

"You ain't got a son like mine." The big man gave a half laugh. "Great lad, but hot headed at times. Got himself into trouble in town last night. I've just been reading him the riot act."

"Got to be done," approved Cap, easing the tension with his approval.

He wanted a calm Mick Owens to talk to, not one whose mind was clouded by anger.

"This is Cap Millett, Mr Owens," said Matt, "friend of the Walters." He turned to Cap. "Cap, this here's Mr Owens."

"Guessed as much," smiled Cap, stepping onto the veranda. "Glad to know you." He extended his hand to the rancher and felt it taken by a broad-fingered grip.

"Mick, please," returned Owens. "Sorry about Doug," he added. "Strange about his disappearance."

"That's what I'd like to talk to you about if you can spare me a few minutes," said Cap.

"Sure," replied Mick. Cap noted the glance of curiosity which Mick gave him as he indicated the chairs on the veranda. "But don't know how I can help."

When the three men were seated, Cap offered an explanation. "You are wondering about me, Mick. My wife,

Laura, and Dorothy were friends way back in Pine Bluffs. We kept in touch spasmodically, but haven't had any news for about two years until Matt here rode with a message from Dorothy telling us about Doug's disappearance and pleading for help. It was a cry we couldn't ignore."

Mick nodded. "I'm sure everything's been done that could be done but as far as I know every line of enquiry has drawn blank." He glanced at Matt for confirmation.

The Circle C rider nodded his agreement.

"I'm sure it has," agreed Cap. "But a fresh mind often sees things differently."

"Too true," said Mick. "And I hope you can find an answer to the riddle of Doug's disappearance. It's sure got me puzzled and I don't see how I can help you."

"Well," said Cap, "there's one question I'd like an answer to. Dorothy tells me that since Doug's disappearance you've offered to buy the Circle C. May I ask why?"

For one moment Mick's face clouded with annoyance but it was gone almost as quickly as it appeared. "Sure," he grinned. "But I assure you I didn't abduct Doug to force Dorothy to sell." Cap raised his hands in a gesture of acceptance, at the same time conveying the impression that he had implied no such thing. "The Circle C is good land, good for cattle and would make a fine addition to the Running W. Doug disappears, seems likely after a while that he may be dead, otherwise why hasn't he turned up? Right, if that's so then the Circle C might just be on the market or coming on the market. If it is, I don't want to miss out so I put in an offer. No harm done if Dorothy doesn't want to sell or if Doug turns up."

"You thought there might be other interested parties and you wanted to be in first?" said Cap.

"Sure there'll be other people

interested. I know for a fact Mel Clancey is. He owns a lot of property in Two Rivers, and I've heard he'd like to expand the town, sees possibilities due to its position. Well, Circle C land very near goes into town, so some of it would help Clancey's plans, but he ain't going to get a piece, he'd have to buy the whole. Now that's just what I don't want to happen, so to forestall any bid by him I put in an offer to Dorothy."

"He's done just that," said Cap.

Though the words were quietly spoken they hit Mick like a clap of thunder.

"The hell he has!" Mick stiffened in his chair. "Hell, I hope Dorothy hasn't accepted."

"No," said Cap. "I can tell you categorically, she hasn't, and at the present time has no intention of selling. She's convinced Doug is still alive."

Mick's relief was obvious. "I hope she's right, I sure do," he said, sinking back in his chair.

"From what you tell me about Clancey, he could have a motive for abducting Doug and then trying to force Dorothy to sell," commented Cap.

"Suppose so," agreed Mick.

"Likely?" asked Cap.

Mick shrugged his shoulders. "Who can tell?"

"Aw, come on, you must have an opinion of the man," pressed Cap.

"Well, he ain't my favourite person," replied Mick. "Too ready to ply my son with liquor and take his money at the tables. I've warned him, but he laughs and asks whether my son's a man or needs a wet-nurse. So I'm biased."

"Toss that aside and give me your thoughts about Clancey," urged Cap.

Mick looked thoughtful for a moment. He frowned and then, a decision made, he looked forcefully at Cap. "Sure, he could just do it, mind you his hands will appear clean. I've nothing on him, but I figure he's behind some deals which have gone a bit near the edge.

He's careful not to buck the law. He's likeable to many, he plays cards right and therefore they see him as good for Two Rivers, but I figure he's out for self and given half the chance will seize the opportunity to hold the town in his pocket and when he does people will pay."

"Where does the law fit in?" asked Cap.

"Sheriff's all right," replied Mick without much enthusiasm.

"You don't seem too keen," prompted Cap.

"Oh, he's all right I suppose," replied Mick. "He keeps things right with the townsfolk but any real trouble always seems to get dealt with by Clancey's side-kicks, the way he wants it."

"So Clancey runs the law in Two Rivers?" said Cap.

"Well, you couldn't come out and say that," said Mick. "You'd have a hard job proving it." Mick glanced at Matt who had quietly listened to the exchanges between the two older men.

"Sure would," agreed Matt. "And you'd have a job to prove that Clancey was playing things dirty."

"What about these side-kicks?" asked Cap.

"Fella name of Shorty Wells runs the show. He moseyed into the town a while back, outsmarted Clancey's troubleshooter and next we knew he was working for Clancey. Tough little bastard, sharp with a gun and quick with his fists," explained Mick.

"Sounds like you've had a run-in with him," observed Cap.

"I ain't but my son, Pete, has and Pete always came off worst and he's no mug when it comes to handling himself. Two more fellas riding for Clancey now. Figure they're pals of Wells, he brought 'em in."

Cap picked up on this information. "So, why does Clancey need more troubleshooters?"

Mick shrugged his shoulders. "Couldn't guess."

Cap looked at Matt who shook

his head. "No idea, unless, following up Mr Owens's observations about expanding the town, he's starting to move that way."

"A point," agreed Cap with a thoughtful quirk to his mouth. "How long have these two been in town?"

"A while, don't know for certain," replied Mick.

"Before Doug's disappearance?" queried Cap.

"Yes," answered Mick. He looked at Cap with a sharp questioning expression. "You don't think . . . ?"

The question was left incomplete but both Cap and Matt read the implication.

"Worth investigating," mused Cap. "Worth investigating."

8

THE following morning Cap sought permission from Clint to have Matt show him the area in which Doug had gone missing.

It was a sharp, clear morning as the two men headed towards the northwest boundaries of the Circle C. The flat, lush grassland gave way to low, rounded hills with the terrain rising steadily towards the foothills of the mountains which formed a majestic, snow-capped backcloth. Cattle grazed peacefully and Cap noted that they were prime stock.

As they climbed, Matt pointed out Two Rivers in the blue distance and Cap could understand Clancey's ambitions to spread the town. The potential of its position close to the confluence of two navigable waterways, albeit for small craft, could be easily seen from the hills. With the added possibility of the railroad coming to Two Rivers, the town could be a goldmine for whoever could utilize its potential.

The more he thought about the situation, the more Cap realized that Clancey had a great deal to gain by getting the Circle C land, but doubt also dogged his mind. Was the incentive big enough for Clancey to risk the repercussions of abducting Doug? If so, then who else might be interested? The mysterious rustler? Had Doug discovered who it was the day he rode out from the Circle C? Or had the man with whom he now rode discovered Doug's real identity and taken revenge for a crime committed five years ago? If so then Matt was a darned good actor at keeping his feelings under control and Cap doubted if he was that.

Cap's speculations were suddenly interrupted when Matt checked his horse with a gasp. "Look!"

Cap stopped his mount and followed the direction of Matt's gaze. A rider topped one of the undulations, rode its ridge momentarily, then disappeared the way he had come.

"Should any Circle C rider be out here?" called Cap.

"None that I know of," replied Matt.

"Let's ride," yelled Cap as he sent his horse into a gallop.

Matt ranged himself alongside Cap and earth tore beneath flying hooves.

Cattle in each hollow reluctantly scurried out of the way of the galloping horses as the two riders made a direct line for the position where the man had appeared. As they started up the final slope, Cap eased the pace and, short of the ridge top, called a halt. The two men slipped from the saddles and crawled quickly to peer over the ridge.

Before them the ground sloped gently into a valley about a mile across before rising more steeply to a rocky terrain with cliff-like outcrops.

A large herd, spread out across

the valley, grazed peacefully. For a moment, Cap and Matt discerned no other movement, then Matt tapped Cap's arm and drew his attention to three horsemen who were driving about a dozen steers away from the main herd.

"Got 'em," hissed Cap. He swung round and scrambled back to his horse.

Matt was close behind as Cap rode cautiously over the ridge and put his horse down the slope. Cap kept the pace steady, his attention on the men ahead.

He sensed the younger man was wanting to make a faster pace, hoping to challenge and catch the rustlers. "Easy, Matt." Cap drew some of the tension away. "We aren't bothered about the cattle. We're more concerned about Doug."

"You think they might lead us to him?" queried Matt, satisfied at Cap's explanation for his steady ride.

"Maybe," replied Cap. "Keep your eyes on them, we don't want to lose them when they reach that rougher terrain."

The two men rode at a pace which gradually closed the gap between themselves and the rustlers without betraying their presence. Cap figured that with their attention on the cattle, the three men would not be too careful about watching their backs.

Cap suddenly called a halt and he and Matt watched as the three men tightened their bunch of cattle and urged them up a rock-strewn slope towards a gap in the high plateau wall.

"Recognize any of them?" asked Cap.

Matt shook his head. "Too far away."

"Know what lies up that slope?" questioned Cap.

"No. Could be a blind canyon. Can't see how there can be a way out," replied Matt.

"Some of these places are a warren. We'll have to take a closer look," said Cap.

They eased their horses forward and kept their eyes on the rustlers.

They saw the three men funnel the cattle through a gap between two huge boulders which, with an upheaval of rocks on either side, all but blocked the entrance to a canyon where the slope levelled out. As the last horseman disappeared, Cap, with a yell of, 'Ride', tapped his horse into a gallop. Matt acted instantaneously and within a few minutes they hit the slope together. They weaved among the boulders, urging their horses upwards.

The pounding of the hooves was suddenly interrupted by the crash of a rifle, its sound, echoing off the towering rock walls, emphasizing its threat. The two horsemen hauled on the reins and, as another bullet whined uncomfortably close, they tumbled out of the saddles and rolled to the cover of some boulders.

Cap cursed. "Damn, should have been more subtle. Should have figured they'd check their tracks before making their final move with the steers."

A bullet ricocheted off the rock behind which he was crouching. He flinched at the closeness of the shot and knew they were up against no mean marksman. He glanced across at Matt who, crouched behind another boulder, had drawn his Colt.

The rifle cracked again, splintering the rock close to Cap. Matt seized the opportunity to peer round his cover to locate the position of the rifleman, only to be sent ducking back by a bullet which clipped the rock near his ear. His lips tightened as he sank back against the boulder. Sweat broke out on his forehead and his hands felt clammy. That had been too close for comfort.

"Hell, he's sure got us pinned down," snapped Matt.

"And he'll keep us here until he knows those steers are safely out of sight."

"You figure they're not just held in a canyon at the top of this slope?" queried Matt, his last words almost lost in the reverberating sound of another rifleshot.

"No," Cap shook his head. "With what they've taken before, there'd be too many to hold so close to the herd. I figure that canyon leads somewhere else."

"And we sure ain't going to find it if this hombre has anything to do with it," muttered Matt. He glanced round desperately. "Any way I can circle him if you give me cover?"

Cap, who had already surveyed their immediate surroundings with that in mind, shook his head. "Forget it, you wouldn't have a chance. The only decent, immediate cover is behind us. I figure we'd best use it to get to our horses and make off."

"What! And let these bastards get away?" Matt was surprised at Cap's apparent defeatist attitude.

"Safety first, Matt . . ."

"But . . . " Matt broke in to protest only to be interrupted by Cap.

"Listen, son, this fella can keep us

pinned here until dark when we'd have no chance of finding where they've taken the cattle. But we can come back tomorrow and scout around, see what we can find."

Matt nodded. "Makes sense," he agreed.

"Right, then let's make this hombre really think he's got us fixed."

Cap poked his hand round the boulder and loosed off a shot in the general direction from which he thought the rifleshots had been coming. Almost immediately the rustler replied with a volley which zipped off both boulders. Matt's answering shot brought another crash of bullets.

Five minutes later Cap once again tested the rustler's reaction and again he was answered by some rapid shooting which kept himself and Matt couched behind their rocks.

"Seems the bastard's bent on keeping us here until dark," muttered Matt.

"That's what I figure, then we have no chance of following him, so I figure we get out of here." Cap glanced round. "Best cover's that way." He indicated the direction to the right.

There was twenty yards of open space to the next huge boulder and from then on Cap had noted they would have cover most of the way back down the slope. On only the odd occasion would they be exposed to a shot and their appearance would be so unexpected that Cap figured they would get clear away to their horses.

"You make the first break, I'll cover you. Then you do the same for me."

Matt nodded.

Cap loosed off two more shots which brought some rapid fire from the rustler. As soon as it finished, Cap called, "Now!"

Matt rose instantly into a crouched run. He broke from the cover and increased his speed. Cap emptied his gun in the direction of the rifleman. He was answered by a volley which after the first three shots turned on the running figure. Bullets clipped the earth close to Matt. He dived the last few yards, flinging himself for the rock cover.

He hit the ground hard, driving the breath from his body. He rolled over and came up against a smaller boulder. He lay for a moment gasping at the air. He was safe. Now for Cap. He pushed himself to his knees and crawled to the bigger boulder. He drew his gun, composed himself and called to Cap. "Ready?"

"A moment," replied Cap. He sat with his back to the rock, recharging the chamber in his Colt from the store of bullets in his gunbelt. Satisfied that he was ready, he scrambled into a crouching position, and noted the space to take him around the other side of the boulder to the path Matt had used. "Coming!" he called and immediately propelled himself forward.

Matt rose above his cover and fired rapidly. He ducked down, flung himself sideways and fired again round the side of the boulder. His action confused the rustler. The first shots of his reply clipped harmlessly at the top of the boulder. His next were directed at the side, with the result that Cap had almost reached the cover before the rustler realized it. He swung his rifle but his final shot was too late, Cap made the position of safety.

"Good work," gasped Cap, as he rolled over beside Matt.

Once they had gathered themselves together, Cap and Matt planned their moves and within a few minutes were making their way down the slope. Cautiously pausing at each space, they then sprinted the few yards to the next cover. Each time their appearance either brought a single shot or none at all. Cap guessed the rustler would be cursing with the frustration of trying to anticipate their next appearance and failing to get in an accurate shot.

Their horses were at the bottom of the slope and Cap knew they would be out of rifle range when they reached them. Breathing heavily from their retreat, the two men soothed the animals and then swung into the saddle.

Cap held his horse steady while he studied the entrance to the canyon. "There must be some way out at the other end," he mused thoughtfully. "Let's ride, Matt, we'll be back tomorrow."

9

AFTER reaching the ranch and having a meal, Cap decided to ride into Two Rivers.

He moved slowly along the main street, casual in the saddle but with his mind alert to everything around him. There was a bustling activity about the town as if it was a place relishing its advantageous position and anticipating a growing future. Three wagons outside the store were being loaded with provisions for three families preparing to find a place to settle further west. The activity around the stage office heralded the departure of the east-bound stage. The sheriff, sitting on a chair outside his office, appeared to be taking little notice of what was happening around him, as if he had seen it all before and everything would proceed normally. The Gilded Cage stood at the corner of the principal crossing with the main street and as Cap brought his horse to a stop outside the saloon he saw that the road to his left led to the river and three landing-stages on which there was activity appertaining to the river craft drawn up against them.

Cap hitched his horse to the rail and stepped on to the sidewalk. He stopped and touched the brim of his stetson to three ladies who hurried by to the emporium a little further along the street. The batwings of The Gilded Cage swung open without a squeak. Two cowboys came out and crossed the street towards the other saloon, Joe's. From the comment which passed between them Cap knew they were anticipating a juicy steak.

Cap entered The Gilded Cage and saw that Clancey had spared nothing to create an atmosphere of satisfying opulence, aimed at making a man feel relaxed and ready to enjoy himself and not count the cost. The gaming tables were in full swing, even at this time of day, encouraging customers to try to make a fortune. Cowboys enjoying time away from their cattle, townsfolk grabbing a few minutes from their job, rivermen having a last throw before heading out of Two Rivers rubbed shoulders at the tables, some encouraged by pretty saloon girls to make a further stake.

Most of the tables in the rest of the saloon were occupied and girls, ready to serve or exchange ribald banter, circulated, making sure the customers were happy. Half a dozen cowboys stood with their beers at the bar. Cap crossed the saloon to the long mahogany counter and called for a beer. The service was quick and amiable and matched the whole atmosphere of friendliness. Cap realized Clancey knew what he was about in the art of persuading men to part with their money.

"New in town?" said the barman, with a friendly nod, as he placed a brimming glass in front of Cap. Cap sensed the eyes weighing him up and reckoned that all newcomers came under a scrutiny which, if it had any element of interest, was reported to Clancey.

"Yes," replied Cap.

"Here for long, or just passing through?" probed the barman.

"Bit of both really," offered Cap. "Shan't be here long, bit of business with Mel Clancey. Told this was his place. Would he be in?"

"I'll find out." The barman moved away. Cap saw him stop at the end of the bar near the stairs. He followed the man's gaze and saw him signal to three men at a table beside the wall at the foot of the stairs and close to a door. Cap moved his position slightly so that he had them within his vision without them being aware that they were under observation. He saw one of the men get up and move to the bar. From his height and broad setting, Cap judged the man to be

Shorty Wells, Clancey's side-kick and no doubt the other two at the table were the recent additions to Clancey's payroll.

The barman and Shorty held a brief but earnest conversation and from the glance in his direction, Cap knew he was the subject of their words. Shorty nodded and straightened from the bar. As he came towards Cap his eyes took in the newcomer but there was nothing familiar about him.

"Howdy," greeted Shorty. "Bert tells me you want to see Mister Clancey."

Cap straightened slowly, eyeing Shorty with an appraising look. "Sure, but I figure you ain't Clancey."

Shorty stiffened. "Right," he replied coldly, "but you can't get to Mister Clancey except through me. So, why do you want to see him?"

"That's my business," replied Cap testily. "If you're his run-around then you toddle off and tell him Cap Millet would like to see him."

Shorty bristled at the put-down. "See

here Millet," he started, anger in his tone.

"No," rapped Cap. "You see here. Tell Clancey I want to see him, anything else is not your concern."

"I make it my concern," hissed Shorty. "No one gets to see Mister Clancey without my approval."

Cap knew Shorty was trying to show his authority, he sensed that attitude in his approach, so Cap was determined to let Shorty and those two hombres sitting with their backs to the wall be fully aware that they were dealing with someone who would stand no nonsense.

"I don't need your approval," snapped Cap, "so git!"

"No, Millet, you git. Out now!" Shorty's eyes flashed towards the batwings.

The tension between the two men had spread to the whole saloon. Conversations had drifted into silence, the gaming tables were still and the cowboys at the bar had slid quietly away from the two protagonists.

Cap gave a half smile of mockery. "I'll go when I've seen Clancey and not before. Now, you either take me to him or tell me where I find him." Cap's eyes were cold. Though his attention was focused on Shorty he was still aware of any movement around him. He had noted that Shorty's two companions had risen to their feet and that their hands hovered near their Colts.

"Like hell I will," rattled Shorty. "Clancey gave me a job to do and I'm doing it."

Cap laughed. "Then he should have given it to someone a bit bigger than you."

Shorty's eyes blazed at the insult. His hand flashed towards his Colt but before his gun cleared leather he found himself staring into the cold muzzle of a Colt.

A low gasp went round the saloon. Folks knew Shorty was fast on the draw and they had thought this stranger was bucking his chances with Clancey's troubleshooter, but now they had seen a man whose draw was lightning. Shorty's gun hadn't even cleared its holster.

"Hold it, you two!" Cap's voice rapped harshly at the two men who had shared Shorty's table. "Shorty wouldn't want you to try it!" Cap's meaning was clear. His cold eyes bore into Shorty. "Turn around."

Shorty glared at Cap then reluctantly shuffled around. His whole body churned with the humiliation. Shown up in front of the whole saloon and especially on his first real encounter since recruiting Dutch and Drew. Shorty's lips tightened. Some day this clever Cap Millet would get his, and he'd take great delight in having him on the wrong end of a gun.

Cap stepped forward, slid Shorty's gun quickly from its holster and pushed it into his own gunbelt. Out of the corner of his eye he saw the barman who had served him start to reach below the counter. "Don't try it!"

The snap in Cap's voice together with its hidden threat startled the barman. "Back off," ordered Cap. The barman and his helpers stepped back and made sure their hands were kept in sight.

"Now, take me to your boss," hissed Cap as he prodded Shorty in the back with his Colt.

Shorty started for the door near the end of the bar. Cap caught the threatening coldness in the eyes of Dutch and Drew as he passed them.

He followed Shorty through the door and found himself in a corridor with a door at the far end which he guessed led outside. Shorty stopped at a door on his right. He glanced at Cap, then knocked. At the call of 'Come in', Shorty opened the door and stepped into the room.

Clancey glanced up from the papers he was examining. His face clouded with an angry surprise when he saw the Colt covering his troubleshooter. "What the hell?" He rose to his feet, cast a glare of annoyance and reprimand at

Shorty before turning his eyes on Cap. "Who the hell are you to come in here at gunpoint?"

"Mel Clancey, I presume?" said Cap calmly.

"Sure," snapped Clancey.

"Cap Millet," Cap introduced himself.

"Never heard of you," rapped Clancey.

"Don't suppose you have, but you have now," drawled Cap.

"So what?" asked Clancey. He was controlling his irritation. This man was cool, steady and he must be fast with a gun to have outdrawn Shorty.

"I asked to see you," explained Cap. "This short tail wanted to know why, said no one got to you except through him. Well, it was none of his business and I only go straight to the top, I never work through any side-kick. Seems he wanted to see if he could beat me to the draw. "You see the result."

Clancey gave a small nod. "All right, Shorty, forget it this time. I'll see Millet."

Shorty accepted the dismissal but the threat behind the glare was not lost on Cap as he left.

Cap smiled to himself. He had hoped to get to Clancey without this trouble but once he had seen it arising he had determined to play tough so that Shorty, his two side-kicks and Clancey would know they were dealing with someone who meant business, for he had a hunch that the reason for Doug's disappearance lay somewhere with these men. Maybe his attitude would make them take actions they would not otherwise make.

Cap slid his Colt back into its holster. He stepped forward as Clancey sat down. "Well, what do you want, Millet?" Clancey asked.

Cap sat down opposite Clancey without being invited. "I'm a friend of Doug Walters. Like to ask you a few questions."

"Why me?" demanded Clancey. "I can't say he was a friend of mine. Came in here very occasionally, wasn't a regular customer by any means."

Cap had been watching the man carefully. He thought that for one very fleeting moment there was a touch of alarm at the mention of Doug, but it was so insignificant that Cap realized he could have been mistaken.

"That as it is," agreed Cap. "But you were interested in making an offer for the Circle C soon after Doug's disappearance; might I ask if you had ever offered to buy from Doug himself?"

Clancey stiffened. "You insinuating that I did and that he turned me down, so I kidnapped him to try to force a sale?" Anger boiled in Clancey's eyes. "You're barking up the wrong tree, Millet. Sure I made an offer to Dorothy. Doug had gone missing. There were people who might be keen to buy his ranch. I was guarding my interests. There's no hiding the fact that I would like to expand this town and having Circle C land would enable me to do just that. This town has a thriving future and those who can see that have a great chance to make money and I'll not deny the fact that that interests me." Clancey's eyes had begun to fire with the desires of an ambitious man and Cap wondered if that driving force could become so absorbing that Clancey would let nothing stand in the way of realizing his desires.

"So you made an offer to Dorothy," said Cap. "Did she turn you down?"

"Sure did. No messing. She believes Doug will turn up," said Clancey and then added contemptuously, "but I guess you knew all that, if you're a friend of Doug then you must have seen Dorothy."

"Sure," replied Cap, "but I wanted to hear it from you. Any idea what might have happened to Doug?"

Clancey shrugged his shoulders. "No. Why should I?"

"You never know," answered Cap.

"See here, Millet. You're insinuating again. You haven't any evidence to attach me to Doug's disappearance, but if you think you have, spit it out." Clancey's eyes narrowed for a moment, but he withdrew the threat which came to his lips.

Cap knew even if Clancey was involved he would not be able to draw him out. The man had completely regained his composure after the initial shock of seeing his side-kick outsmarted. Now he was playing things cool.

Cap pushed himself from the chair. "Thanks for your time," he said smoothly. "Sorry we had to meet this way. If you hear any talk in the saloon about Doug's disappearance I'm sure you'll let me or Dorothy know. I'm staying at the Circle C."

"You can rely on me. It must be worrying for her." All the usual shrewd suavity was back and Cap recognized a man who was cunning, one not to be underestimated, a man who would do anything, use anybody, to achieve his ambitions.

Cap was halfway to the door when he stopped and turned. "By the way,

Clancey, you interested in cows and ranching?"

Clancey gave a short laugh. "Do I look like I am?" He spread his arms in a gesture to his surroundings.

Cap returned his laugh. "Guess not."

When Cap stepped into the saloon, Shorty was sitting at the table with Dutch and Drew. Cap stopped, took Shorty's gun from his belt and dropped it on the table. "Guess you look a bit naked without this, shorttail. Next time I'll go straight in to see Mister Clancey, so don't get in my way." Cap glanced at Shorty's two companions. "That goes for you two as well."

Dutch stiffened as if he would retaliate but Drew laid a restraining hand on his arm. "Easy," he hissed. "Your time will come."

10

"HEARD you outsmarted Shorty Wells yesterday afternoon," commented Matt as he and Cap rode away from the ranch bound for the canyon where they had last seen the rustlers.

Cap shot him a glance. "Where'd you hear that?"

"Couple of the boys and I rode into town yesterday evening. Had a couple of drinks in The Gilded Cage. The place was buzzing with the news, and I'll tell you, Shorty was none too pleased with some of the remarks that were made. You sure showed him up. Reckon you'd better watch your back."

"You reckon?" said Cap quizzically.

"Sure do. Shorty can be real mean, and he won't forget what you did. Why did you buck him? Thought you'd have kept a low profile."

"I reckoned just seeing Clancey was raising my profile, so I figured on letting his side-kicks and himself know they were dealing with someone who didn't mind trouble. Might make them anxious about their situation and they might show some of their cards."

"Then you think Clancey might be behind Doug's disappearance?" pressed Matt.

"Let's just say I have feeling about that set-up," answered Cap, easing himself in the saddle. "Those two fellas Shorty brought in look hardcases, wish I knew more about them."

Matt shrugged his shoulders. "You know how it is, folks don't ask too many questions around Shorty."

Cap nodded. They rode for a while in silence until Cap drew his horse to a halt. Matt stopped alongside, followed Cap's intense gaze and realized he was studying the approach to the canyon. Not wanting to break Cap's concentration, Matt sat still and held his mount steady.

After five minutes Cap straightened, a sign that his study was over. He glanced at Matt. "Can't be dead certain but I figure there's no one up there." He looked back at the approach to the canyon where they had been forced to turn back yesterday. "Let's ride." He quickened the pace, knowing that he and Matt would be pleased to find some respite from the intensifying heat of the sun in the shadow of the canyon walls.

Cattle eyed them curiously for a moment or ignored them completely as they crossed the grassland. This gave way to thin scrub which surrendered to the rocky surface as they climbed towards the canyon. The two riders gentled their horses upwards, threading their way around huge boulders and gingerly crossing slabs of flat rock.

Reaching the entrance to the canyon, Cap stopped. Once more he studied the way ahead. Great walls of rock, split, cut, and scarred, towered on either side. The sun touched the top of the canyon flaming the rock into yellows and browns, contrasting sharply with the subdued light and colours lower down. The faint sighing of the air in the upper reaches of the canyon seemed to emphasize the silence rather than detract from it. Nothing moved.

Cap's horse stirred. He leaned forward and patted it comfortingly on the neck. He glanced at Matt. "Well I reckon we'll find neither man or beast in here. I reckon this is a blind canyon."

"But where the hell could they go?" said Matt. "They were heading for here before they knew we were on their trail, so they weren't just going to hold the cattle here until they'd got rid of us. They came here for a purpose."

"Right," agreed Cap. "Then let's take a look."

The two men tapped their horses forward. The animals, though uneasy about going further into the canyon, were reassured by their riders' comforting presence.

They worked their way slowly deeper and deeper into the canyon until the walls on either side began to close in on them and they saw the huge barrier of solid rock ahead.

Puzzled, the two riders stopped. Cap tipped his stetson with his forefinger and scratched his temple. He shook his head as he readjusted his headgear. "Where the hell could they go?" he muttered between clenched teeth. He looked around him, irritated as he seemed to hear the walls of rock mock him with a challenge: *I've a secret, find it if you can.*

"Matt, we'll work our way back examining the rock face more closely. You take the right side, I'll take the left."

"But we saw nothing," replied Matt.

"I know, but those steers must have gone somewhere," said Cap. "Come on, let's try." He slipped from the saddle and led his horse to the left side of the canyon.

Matt turned his horse and rode to

the wall of the rock before swinging to the ground.

The two men worked their way back along the canyon examining every cutting which marred the smooth rock face. Frustration mounted with every step and, after twenty minutes, Cap was beginning to despair when a shout from Matt gave him renewed hope.

"Cap, get over here!" There was a touch of excitement in Matt's voice.

Cap left his horse and hurried across the canyon.

"Look, here, Cap," urged Matt. He indicated a towering cut in the rock which ran along the rock face parallel to the canyon itself. "It appears to be just a slit in the rock," explained Matt, "but on closer examination it widens before narrowing again. I reckon it might be worth looking further but figured I should get you first."

"Good man." Cap slapped Matt on the shoulder. There was a new enthusiasm in his voice when he said, "Let's go."

Matt left his horse and the two men entered the slit with Cap leading.

"Just enough room for a steer or a horse to get through," commented Cap. "Let's hope it leads somewhere." He hurried on. The slit widened and Cap moved into a brighter space. He looked up and far, far above he saw blue sky. The rock was split right up to the top of the plateau.

"This is as far as I went," explained Matt. "As you can see the slit narrows again after this." He nodded in the direction in which they were going.

Cap hurried across the intervening space but his heart sank when he realized that the opening was now so narrow that there was no way a steer could be driven through it.

He turned back with a curse. "Damn, I figured we had found it." Cap and Matt were downcast.

"Reckon we'll have to start again," muttered Matt.

They had reached the wider part of the slit. Cap stopped and looked around. The ground was strewn with boulders, some so large that they hid the immediate rock face.

"Let's take a look here," he suggested.

The two men started to examine the rock face wherever it seemed possible for steers to get behind an intervening boulder.

Five minutes later an exuberant shout from Cap took Matt hurrying round a huge boulder to find no sign of him. He stared in amazement for a moment then realized he was looking into a huge cave.

"You in there, Cap?" he called.

His voice boomed into the void and brought an equally echoing response.

"In here, Matt!"

Matt moved forward carefully. It was gloomy, the roof lowered but remained high enough for him to walk upright, and way in the distance there was a faint light — the end of the cave-like tunnel. A few moments later he made out the silhouetted form of Cap, still moving forward. Matt followed. He saw Cap reach the end of the tunnel and stop. Matt quickened his pace. There was no shout of triumph from Cap but Matt sensed that the older man had discovered something and was waiting for him to discover it too.

Panting, Matt scrambled the last few yards to Cap and, as he came out into the daylight, he gasped with surprise.

Here was a small valley, about a mile long and half a mile wide locked in by towering walls of rock. There was sufficient feed for a few cattle and running water from a stream which entered and left the valley below the rock wall at each end.

A small stone hut with an earth roof stood at the far end of the valley but there was no sign of life and the place was empty of cattle.

"Reckon we've found it!" said Cap enthusiastically.

"But there's no one here." There was a note of disappointment in Matt's voice, who had hoped to catch the rustlers red-handed.

"No, but this place was only to hold the cattle for very short periods of time, it couldn't support many," said Cap. "But, look. That's the way they take them out of this valley." He indicated a trail which twisted up the lowest part of the rock face, at the opposite end of the valley close behind the hut, before crossing a ridge.

"Got it!" cried Matt excitedly. "We want our horses!"

Both men hurried back the way they had come. Once they had collected their mounts, and cajoled them with gentle words and urgings when they were reluctant to face the unfamiliar parts of the route, they rode quickly across the valley to the hut.

It only needed a cursory look round to see that it had been occupied very recently, more than likely for the one night — last night. Cap held his hand over the ashes in the grate. There was still a slight warmth about them.

"They've been here the night and

moved the cattle out this morning," said Cap.

"Then we could pick up their trail," enthused Matt.

The two men hurried from the hut and put their mounts at the trail to the ridge. As they climbed they saw evidence of the trail having been used recently by cattle and horses. They pressed on, urging their mounts, eager to see what would be revealed when they reached the ridge.

Their immediate reaction was disappointment for before them stretched a flat tableland of dry scrub, bound on each side by precipitous cliffs of varying height. However the trail taken by the rustlers was easy to follow and Cap and Matt set their horses to follow it. They rode for about two miles before the landscape changed, with the cliffs on each side lowering to merge with the land on which they were riding. The whole gave way to a gentle slope and at the top of the slope the two men reined in their horses.

Matt let out a low whistle of surprise. Below them, running at right angles to their position, was a valley of lush grassland. It was surrounded by terrain similar to that on which they were standing, making it a hidden valley. A partially constructed house lay at one end, with other buildings close by. Cattle grazed peacefully along the valley.

The two men automatically pulled their horses back from the edge of the slope, slid from the saddles and crept back until they could view the valley.

"Reckon you're looking at Circle C steers," commented Cap. "But I figure you'll never prove it. Easy brand to change. I reckon you'll find they're now Circle O, and I'll guess those are the steers we saw rustled." Cap nodded in the direction of a corral close to the house where branding was taking place.

"Let's get 'em," cried Matt, anxious to uncloak the rustlers' activities.

"Hold it, Matt," called Cap. "You'd

never make it in time. See, they've only four more left to do. There'd be nothing to say they weren't Circle O cattle."

Matt nodded. "Guess you're right." A despondent note had crept into his voice.

Cap smiled at how quickly the enthusiasm of the young could be turned the other way. "Well, Matt, we've uncovered something here, something which may lead us to Doug. Don't forget he's our prime concern. Did you know this valley existed?"

"No, never had cause to explore the mountains," replied Matt.

"Can you figure out exactly where we are?" asked Cap. "There must be another way out of this valley."

"Not sure," mused Matt. He studied the terrain and the position of the sun. "Two Rivers will be over there." He indicated to his right. "That stream seems to disappear under those hills, reckon it must reappear at the other side and join the river which forms the left-hand fork at Two Rivers."

"This valley is hidden from that river," commented Cap, "so there's only a few folk know of its existence. Mmm, an ideal place for rustled cattle. Look." He pointed towards the hills just to the right of a point where the stream went underground. "That looks like a pass through the hills."

"You're right," agreed Matt. "So the rustled cattle are brought here, brand changed, held here until the right time, taken through that pass, then across the river and then well, could be anywhere." He glanced at Cap. "What now? Do you think there's a link between Doug's disappearance and the rustling?"

"Could be. Doug may have come across the rustlers that day, like we did, but maybe he wasn't as lucky as we were," commented Cap.

"Then," Matt hesitated, fearing to voice the worst.

"Sure, they may have killed him and we may never find his body, could be anywhere, there's a warren of cuttings and blind canyons around here. But I just have a hunch there may be more to it. I can't tie Clancey and his side-kicks in with rustling, they aren't the ranching sort. Don't give the appearance of having been around cattle much."

"But Clancey could be behind it, getting someone else to do the rustling to try to force a sale of the Circle C," pointed out Matt.

"You could be right," agreed Cap.

"So what do we do now?" pressed Matt.

"Let's see what happens," said Cap. "The branding's finished." All the time they had been speaking Cap had been watching the activity and studying the buildings. "You know, Matt, I reckon none of those buildings are habitable yet."

Matt surveyed the constructions more thoroughly. "Guess you're right, Cap. I figure someone is planning to use this valley as a thriving ranch built up on someone else's cattle. But who? Reckon we'll find out if we take a look round down there?"

"Possible," agreed Cap.

"Then let's go," urged Matt. "We can work round towards the buildings, there's plenty of cover along the hillside."

He started to scramble to his feet but Cap dragged him back down.

"Hold it, Matt. Whatever happens we don't want to be seen. Might push them into doing something with Doug and that we don't want to happen."

"But we don't know if Doug's disappearance has anything to do with the rustling," said Malt.

"True," agreed Cap. "But I reckon they're tied up." He eyed the buildings again. "I reckon those hombres down there will ride out, those buildings aren't habitable yet, then we can take a closer look."

The two men settled down to wait. Half an hour later four men came out from one of the buildings, went round the back and a few minutes later reappeared on horseback, leading the fifth horse, saddled. They came to the front of the main building and waited. Barely half a minute had passed when a man came out, stepped down from the half-constructed veranda and mounted the fifth horse. He sent it forward and as they headed along the valley the other riders fell in behind him.

"Brent Morrison!" The gasp came from Matt.

Cap cast him a sharp look. "Doug's ex-foreman? You sure?"

"Certain," confirmed Matt. "He's a big man, and I'd know his sit on a horse anywhere."

"Morrison trying to set up his own ranch at the expense of the Circle C?" mused Cap. "Maybe Clancey isn't behind the rustling, only taking advantage of it to try to get the Circle C. This may be the break we want. Let's tail 'em."

"You don't think Doug's down there?" asked Matt, a note of urgency in his voice at the thought that if they rode away they might be losing the chance of finding his boss.

"We'll cover both options," replied Cap. "You take a look down there, I'll tail Morrison. See you back at the Circle C."

11

THE rustlers were halfway along the valley when Cap crossed the ridge and put his horse down the slope. They were heading for the section of the hills which Cap had identified as a pass out of the valley.

He matched his pace to the riders ahead, using what cover he could, but once they had moved into the pass he quickened his pace. Whatever happened he did not want to lose them.

Reaching the hills he steadied his pace again and proceeded with every nerve alert. He guessed the rustlers would have ridden straight through but he had to be cautious. The hills closed in, the pass narrowed. He was aware of the sound of his horse's hooves echoing from the rock face. He stopped and listened. Silence had descended on the pass. The riders must be through, unless . . .

But he must not lose them. This might be the chance he wanted. He sent his horse forward quickly, ignoring the sound he was making, ignoring the chance of an ambush, banking on the certainty that the riders were not aware of his presence.

He reached the far end of the pass to find himself at the top of a long decline, with the hills on either side gradually descending to a wide valley through which flowed the river Matt had mentioned.

The five riders had increased their pace and were already moving out into the valley towards the river. Cap saw them turn downstream and knew they must be heading for Two Rivers. He needed to close the gap otherwise he might lose them. He weighed up the terrain in a swift appraisal and turned his horse across the hillside so that he could cut at a tangent to the trail taken by the men he tailed.

Reaching the river-bank he matched his speed to that of the rustlers. When Two Rivers came in sight the five men halted. After a brief conversation two of them put their mounts at the river where it ran with less depth. Two others rode on. Cap guessed they were going to use the other ford in order to reach the town. Brent Morrison remained where he was, relaxed in the saddle, and rolled himself a smoke.

Cap smiled to himself. These men obviously didn't want to be seen riding into Two Rivers together and Brent Morrison wanted to arrive on his own. Well, that suited him very well. It was Brent he wanted to tail.

Brent finished his smoke, flicked the stub into the river, settled himself in the saddle and sent his horse forward. He kept to a walking pace alongside the river until he reached a point about a quarter of a mile downstream from the confluence of the two rivers. He put his animal at the water. The horse hesitated for a moment, then, cajoled gently by its rider, carefully stepped over the stones and entered the river.

Hidden by a clump of trees, Cap watched. He saw the water gradually get deeper to a point halfway across the river. There Brent halted and seemed to survey the water ahead for a moment, before urging the horse on. The horse plunged into the water and swam strongly for the opposite bank.

Cap was glad he had seen this for he would have been caught unawares by the sudden deepening of the river. Now he realized that there had to be some depth to the river for boats to reach the town.

He watched Brent emerge from the water. Relieved to be away from the drag of the river the animal stopped and shook itself before answering its rider's call to move. Brent turned the animal in the direction of Two Rivers.

Cap waited but still had Brent in sight when he crossed the river. He wasted no time in following, and saw Morrison take a back street which ran parallel to the main street. Cap now urged caution, for the street was quiet. There was little to attract people to it. To the right were the backs of the buildings which fronted the main street, while the left-hand side was occupied with storehouses, the odd stable and only a couple of blocks which could be termed dwellings.

Cap slid from his horse and led it into the first alley. From the corner he saw Brent Morrison leading his horse into a building on the left-hand side of the street which Cap estimated to be a stable. A few moments later Morrison reappeared and entered a building next to the stable. Cap waited. After ten minutes of turning over alternative courses of action, and beginning to favour a confrontation with Morrison, Cap's thoughts were interrupted by the sight of Morrison, in a change of clothing, crossing the street to the back of The Gilded Cage.

Cap's thoughts raced. Morrison using the back door. He could get directly to

Clancey and no one would know. Was Clancey behind rustling? Was Morrison reporting the latest state of play? Had Clancey ordered Doug's abduction to bring pressure to bear on Dorothy? There were so many possibilities that Cap could reach no conclusion. How he wished he could hear what was being said in The Gilded Cage. Formulating his next move in his mind, Cap, having decided to tail Morrison another day, was about to move away when the back door of The Gilded Cage opened. Morrison came out and crossed to the dwelling opposite. Cap decided to wait to see if there were any further developments.

Five minutes later Drew and Dutch came from the saloon and hurried across the street to the building which Brent had entered.

Excitement gripped Cap. Was this the lead he needed? Were Dutch and Drew tied in with Morrison? They weren't cattlemen and Cap couldn't see them on a working ranch. Maybe they were just keeping an eye on Morrison and his operation for Clancey. After all they were his troubleshooters. Or were they in league with Morrison without Clancey's knowledge?

Cap slipped from the alley and hurried quietly to the house occupied by Morrison. House? Cap realized it was little more than a shack, a place which a man might use as a temporary measure. He flattened himself against the wall and edged towards the window. Voices came to him but were not clear enough for him to hear what was being said.

A quick glance through the window showed him that the shack consisted of one room and that the three men were sitting at a table towards the rear. Cap moved quickly but silently to the back of the building where he had noticed a window partially open.

As he moved closer to the window the voices became more distinguishable.

"How long does Clancey want you to keep up with the rustling, Brent?"

"Until Dorothy Walters' position is

weak enough for her to sell the Circle C to him. And he's pressing me to take more cattle at a time."

"Don't be over-anxious to make a big raid yet."

"I'm not. I want a way out if I can work one. This thing's got bigger and gone further than I ever intended. I was just taking a few cattle for myself after I'd discovered that valley. Figured I'd set myself up there, but Clancey found out what I was doing and blackmailed me into working it to his advantage. Then Shorty brought you boys along."

"And your rustling provided a nice blind for us to take Doug Walters." A laugh accompanied the observation.

"Was that Clancey's idea? To bring more pressure to bear on the Walters to sell the ranch?"

"No. Walters' kidnapping has nothing to do with Clancey."

Cap's mind was absorbing the information. So Doug had been abducted; Clancey was clear of that but was pleased to use it to pressurize Dorothy.

"Then what's your interest in him?" asked Brent.

"No concern of yours." The voice was cautious but behind it was the chill of warning. "Keep your nose out of our business. Don't worry, you'll get well paid for providing the opportunity to get Walters and giving us an ideal place to hide him."

Excitement gripped Cap. Doug was still alive!

"I'd like him cleared soon," said Brent. "I don't like being mixed up with kidnapping."

"You ain't, so forget it. I reckon we can make Walters see our point of view in a couple of days."

"Where does Shorty fit in?" asked Morrison. "He brought you here."

"We said, don't be nosey."

Cap slipped quietly away to his horse. He had the information he wanted. But what was Dutch and Drew's game? What interest had they in Doug? Dutch? Drew? The realization so startled Cap that he pulled his horse to a halt. Dutch Lowry and Drew Rogers? Could they be Dutch Hardy and Drew Kinkaid, the two members of the Fenton gang, apart from Doug, who had escaped? Had they changed their surnames but foolishly kept their Christian names, unlike Doug who had changed them both and lost his identity? If they were, how had they found Doug? Then Cap remembered that it was Shorty who had brought them to Two Rivers on the pretext of Clancey wanting more troubleshooters. Did Shorty know who Doug really was? And how had he known where to find Dutch Hardy and Drew Kinkaid? The only reason he would bring them would be for his own ends — part of the bank cash which, as far as anyone knew, had never been returned.

He figured he was near a lot of answers. Finding Doug was his first concern and the best way he could do that was through Dutch and Drew for they had indicated they would be dealing with Doug again in the next two days. He also realized that to keep Doug's true identity a secret he would have to act on his own. He could not enlist anyone else's help, especially Matt's after his threat of what he would do if he ever came across the survivors of the Fenton gang.

But his immediate concern was to relieve Dorothy's mind. Cap put his horse to a gallop and headed for the Circle C.

12

CAP'S rapid approach to the ranchhouse brought Dorothy and Laura hurrying out of the house to meet him.

"Doug's alive!" he called as he brought his mount to a dust-stirring halt.

The shock of such good news froze Dorothy's immediate reaction for a fraction of a second, then one word burst from her lips. "Where?"

Joy at the news brought laughter mingling with jubilation and relief to Laura's eyes.

Cap was out of the saddle and leaping up the steps. "I'm sorry, I don't know."

Dorothy's delight turned to bewilderment amidst tears of happiness. "But I don't . . . How do you know Doug's alive?" Dorothy looked pleadingly at

Laura as if seeking her help to solve the mystery.

Laura frowned. What did her husband mean? How could he know Doug was alive and yet not know where he was? She glanced at him, demanding a quick explanation.

"I think you'd better sit down while I explain," he said gently. He took Dorothy's arm and turned her to a chair. She sat down and Laura sat next to her, while Cap sank onto a bench opposite them with his back to the veranda railing.

"All I am going to tell you at this stage is that I know Doug is alive. Where, I don't know but I aim to find out."

"But how did you find out?" queried Dorothy.

"That I am not prepared to tell you yet," returned Cap quietly. He did not want to upset Dorothy by telling her that he believed two of the Fenton gang had Doug.

"Cap!" admonished Laura.

"Please!" cried Dorothy.

"I'm sorry, but I think it wisest that you don't know how I found out," replied Cap. "Not yet."

"But why?" pleaded Dorothy.

"Please, don't press me," said Cap. "Just be happy that he's alive."

"Oh, I am, Cap, I am." Dorothy jumped from her chair and flung her arms round Cap's neck. She hugged him tightly. "I'm so grateful to you Cap. Thank you for what you've done."

Cap smiled and then assumed a more serious attitude as Dorothy remained on the seat beside him. "Save your thanks until I have Doug safely back on this veranda."

"But you don't think . . . ?" started Laura.

"No, everything will be all right," he said, to ease the alarm on the faces of the two friends. "Oh, I don't want you to tell anyone about this."

"But shouldn't we tell the crew? They're anxious about Doug," said Dorothy.

"No," said Cap firmly. "If anyone else knows it could jeopardize things. I couldn't keep my news from you, but I don't want anyone else to know just yet. Promise me."

Dorothy and Laura nodded.

"Good. We've . . . oh, by the way, is Matt back yet?"

"I haven't seen him," replied Dorothy.

"Didn't he ride out with you?" asked Laura.

"Yes, but we split up," explained Cap.

"And it was after that that you learned Doug is alive?" suggested Laura.

"Yes."

"So Matt doesn't know," said Dorothy.

"No. And no one must know," Cap insisted decisively once again. "Not even Matt." He gave a slight pause to emphasize his insistence, then went on. "We located the rustled cattle."

"Where?" gasped Dorothy.

"Secret valley in the mountains," replied Cap.

"Know the rustlers?" asked Dorothy.

"Brent Morrison."

"Might have guessed, after we sacked him." Dorothy's lips tightened with annoyance.

"You were losing cattle before that," pointed out Cap, "so it wasn't done out of revenge. I figure he'd come across this valley, it's good for cattle, and decided to make his spread with cattle from your herds. But I believe it gets more complicated than that."

"How so?" asked Dorothy. "Someone else involved? Mike Owens? Mel Clancey? They both wanted to buy me out."

"Not Mike." Cap shook his head. "He's in the clear."

"Clancey, then?"

"I figure he's involved, but mainly to try to pressurize you into selling."

"And he instigated the kidnapping to bring more pressure," cried Dorothy.

"No. I don't think he was behind

the kidnapping. I don't think he knows anything about it," explained Cap.

"Then who?" There was a pleading cry to know in Dorothy's voice.

"I can't tell you," replied Cap.

"But you know?" queried Laura.

"I think I do, but I'm not sure," said Cap. "Now, no more questions. And remember, you know nothing." Cap had spied Matt heading for the Circle C.

Seeing Cap's horse, Matt headed straight for the ranchhouse.

"Find anything?" called Cap as Matt brought his horse to a halt.

"Not really," replied Matt, swinging from the saddle. There was a touch of disappointment in his voice. He glanced at Dorothy and Laura as he came onto the veranda and, not knowing what Cap had told them, cast a querying look at him.

"I've told them we've found the cattle and that Brent Morrison's doing the rustling," explained Cap. "Did you find any trace of Doug?"

"None," replied Matt. "Those buildings appeared to be used just temporary, but there was every indication that they're going to become permanent. Brent Morrison setting himself up."

"What are we going to do about him, Cap?" asked Dorothy, realizing that she should show some concern in front of Matt.

"Nothing at the moment," replied Cap. "If we do, we might jeopardize finding Doug. I don't say Morrison's connected with Doug's disappearance but you never know."

"Didn't you come up with anything?" asked Matt.

"Nothing," returned Cap. "Morrison and his cowboys rode into Two Rivers."

Matt's lips tightened but his mind was puzzled. He felt Cap was holding something back and he sensed that there was less tension in these three friends, especially in Dorothy. Since Doug's disappearance she had naturally been uptight, worried, anxious, concerned

— all of which had been reflected in her physical appearance. But now she seemed a little more relaxed, as if some news had eased the distress. And he figured the news, to have such an effect, must concern Doug. But why hold back? Why not tell him? What did they not want him to know?

He was all the more puzzled the next morning when, expecting to ride with Cap again, he was sent by his foreman to check on the herd from which the cattle had been rustled. It seemed a job for nothing, for he didn't expect the rustlers to strike again so soon.

As he left the ranch, he paused on a rise and looked back. A rider, whom he identified as Cap, was heading for Two Rivers. Matt shrugged his shoulders and rode on.

13

REACHING Two Rivers, Cap swung from the saddle outside The Gilded Cage. As he crossed to the bar he noticed Shorty and Dutch sitting at their usual table. He wondered where Drew could be and wished he knew. He wanted all three men in sight. Sipping his beer he was aware that he had come under the observation of the two men. Cap pushed himself from the counter and, with his unfinished drink, meandered casually to the gaming tables and stood watching a game of poker, in a position from which he still had the two men in view.

After twenty minutes he saw Drew come through the doorway beside the table, have a brief word with Dutch and Shorty and then leave again. A few minutes later, Dutch and Shorty left the same way. Cap drained his drink and left the saloon. Once on the boardwalk he moved quickly to the side road, but without the haste which draws attention, and then headed towards the back street.

Before he reached the corner, four riders appeared. He drew back quickly against the wall of the saloon and observed Dutch, Drew, Shorty and Morrison keeping to the back street as if they were heading out of town.

Cap's pulse beat quicker. Were they heading for the secret valley? More than likely, since they had Morrison along. If so were they going to implement the threat he had overheard them make against Doug?

Cap hurried back to the main street, untied his horse and swung into the saddle. He sent the animal at a trot along the dusty roadway, easing the pace when he neared the end of the street. Before he reached the edge of town, the four riders came within his vision. He halted and kept them under surveillance.

The men appeared to be riding with a purpose. They were moving at a steady clip but without undue haste. There was a determined set about them, as if they were bound on a mission, the outcome of which could be in their favour.

They crossed the river and from the direction they took Cap felt certain they were heading for Morrison's valley.

When Cap judged it right to break cover, he headed for the ford. By the time he reached the opposite bank the four riders were mere dots in the distance.

He followed at a decreet distance so as not to draw attention to himself. When he felt certain that the riders were heading for the hidden valley he cut across country and positioned himself out of sight above the pass into the valley, from where he watched their steady progress. There was no urgency about their ride, but they still held that purposeful pace.

Cap watched them negotiate the pass until they were out of sight. He remounted his horse and set it down the slope towards the head of the pass. He negotiated the incline without any trouble and halted when he could see into the valley. The riders were steadying their horses down the final section of the trail to the valley floor. He watched them top a small rise and disappear over the side before he sent his horse down the trail. Short of the top of the rise, Cap slid from the saddle and scrambled the last few yards on foot. He flattened himself on the ground and peered over the ridge.

His lips tightened with annoyance. The riders must have quickened their pace once over the rise for now they were mere dots among the rough terrain at the far end of the valley, beyond the half-completed buildings.

Only two! Where were the others? Another one! Three! Now two! Now three! The riders twisted amongst the boulders. Cap could not be sure if he had seen them all, they were too far away to identify individually, but he felt he must have done for he saw no reason why they should split up. There was certainly no sign of any one of them along the valley.

Cap hurried back to his horse. He must not lose sight of them.

★ ★ ★

Matt rode among the cattle. They were quietly grazing. Everything seemed usual and there was no sign of any other human being. Normally Matt would have enjoyed riding herd. He loved it out here, the space, the big sky and the far horizon. But today he felt uneasy, annoyed that, suddenly, he seemed to have been left out of Cap's search for Doug. He still wondered about the atmosphere he had sensed on seeing Cap, Dorothy and Laura when he had returned yesterday. The heavy anxiety had been missing. Did they know something which they did not want him to know? If so, what? And why keep it a secret? And why did he feel he had been deliberately left out of Cap's plans for today?

He was puzzled but he had a feeling that the answers lay somewhere in the valley which he and Cap had discovered yesterday. But where? He had made a search around the buildings but discovered nothing. Had he overlooked a clue? Would it be worth taking another look? The cattle were grazing quietly. There was nothing for him to do here. He figured the rustlers were not likely to return today, so there would be no harm in him riding to the valley again.

He turned his horse to the high country and moved it into a canter. Reaching the slope to the canyon he steadied the horse to a walk and once he reached the cleft in the rock he swung from the saddle and led it on foot. Before he emerged on the overlook of the valley Matt secured his horse out of sight.

From his position above the valley, Matt surveyed the terrain for twenty minutes. There was no movement apart from the cattle grazing contentedly. There was no one at the buildings and nothing marred the peaceful scene. He had searched the buildings yesterday and found no sign to indicate that Doug had been there. If Morrison had abducted him then he had him elsewhere. Maybe it would be worth exploring the valley still further.

As he turned to go for his horse a movement at the far end of the valley caught his eye. He waited. Riders! Four of them. He watched their progress along the valley. He lost sight of them behind a ridge, then saw them cross and put their horses into a faster gait.

When they came into a recognizable distance, Matt felt tension grip him. His fists clenched and his breath came faster. Morrison, Shorty, Dutch and Drew! If Clancey's troubleshooters were riding with Morrison was the saloon owner behind the rustling?

As the riders neared the buildings, Matt saw Morrison break away and head towards the unfinished constructions. The other three continued riding towards the uneven terrain at the head of the valley. Where were they going and why? Had they anything to do with Doug's disappearance? Were they acting on orders from Clancey? Questions poured into his mind and he had to find the answers, but could he get past the buildings without being seen by Morrison, who had taken his horse into what Matt reckoned had to be a stable?

He studied the land to his left and figured that if he kept close to the top of the slope, near the soaring rock face of the plateau, he might be able to keep out of sight.

He turned to go when he was brought up short by the sight of another rider topping the rise in the valley.

Matt's lips tightened with frustration. If he rode out now he might be seen, yet if he waited he could lose the three riders he was desperate to follow. He eyed the lone rider again. The horse moved faster. Trying to catch up or following? A member of the rustling gang or . . . ?

Matt's thoughts exploded with the moment of recognition. Cap Millet! What the hell was he doing here? Had he gone to town knowing something which necessitated keeping a watch on the men who had ridden along the valley? What did Cap know or suspect, that he did not?

Matt watched. Cap was riding openly, not trying to disguise his presence from anyone who might be at the half-constructed buildings. Matt stiffened with a touch of anxiety. Maybe Cap did not know that Brent had left the other three. Matt weighed up distances. Cap could have been at the far side of the rise when Brent deviated his ride. If so then Brent would soon be aware of Cap's approach.

Matt concentrated on the buildings, watching for the slightest sign of Brent's intentions. A few minutes later he saw Brent come to the door of the ranchhouse and peer in Cap's direction. He ducked back out of sight but Matt had the feeling that he was still watching.

Cap passed the buildings without giving them a second glance. His concentration was focused on the rough country ahead, and Matt judged that he had some riders still in sight. Once Cap was safely past the buildings, Matt saw Brent slip from the house and hurry to the stable. A few moments later he rode out, cautiously observed the route taken by Cap, and then sent his horse to follow.

Matt hurried to his horse, swung into the saddle and turned along the hillside above the valley, cutting at an angle which would bring him on to the same trail as that taken by Brent.

Reaching the trail he saw no sign of Cap, nor of the three riders Cap was following. He only just glimpsed Brent Morrison starting to thread his way across the boulder-strewn slope. Matt urged his horse forward. Whatever happened he must not lose contact. He sensed Cap was in danger and that somewhere ahead lay the answer to Doug's disappearance.

14

CAP pulled his horse to a halt. Three riders ahead were emerging on to a clear path which ran straight towards what he judged to be a large cave in the rock wall soaring to the plateau surrounding the hidden valley.

Three! Where was the fourth? Puzzled, Cap waited. He identified the men ahead: Shorty, Dutch, Drew. Where was Morrison? Cap's lips tightened. He cursed himself for being careless. If Brent wasn't with the others then maybe he had stopped off at the ranchhouse, in which case he must have been aware of Cap's presence for he had not attempted to disguise it when he passed the buildings. Morrison could well be behind him, tailing him. Now he would have to watch his back as well as keeping an eye on the men he felt sure were going to lead him to Doug.

Cap surveyed the terrain ahead. By using the boulder cover on either side of the path he could easily move towards the cave but he would have to leave his horse, and he had Brent Morrison somewhere behind him.

He swung from his saddle and led his mount to his left to a hollow hidden from the path. After securing the animal he hurried at a half-run back towards the track. Brent must not be allowed to ride straight through to warn the others. With gun drawn he waited behind a huge boulder.

Time dragged. Cap champed with irritation. He wanted to get on, wanted to know if Doug was in the cave, needed to find out what was happening. But where was Morrison? The only way he could ride to the cave was along the path. But had he left his horse and slipped by on foot? Were all four of them, at this moment, just waiting for him, ready to shoot him down? Or was Morrison covering him at this very moment, his finger hooked around a trigger?

Cap licked his dry lips. He glanced round nervously. No sign of anyone. He cooled his racing thoughts. He wasn't certain that Brent had followed him but it seemed more than likely. Irritated, Cap decided he could wait no longer.

He had to know what was happening at the cave. If Doug was there his life could be in danger. Cap edged round the boulder and moved quickly to the next cover. He paused for a moment catching his breath and in that instant heard a foot scrape on the rock. He swung round quickly, his gun menacing, but he found himself staring into the cold muzzle of a Colt ready to blast his stomach wide open.

"Who the hell are you and what are you doing here?" Brent Morrison snapped. There was cold threatening menace in his eyes.

It was only as the words were spoken

that Cap realized that he and Morrison had never come face to face. Maybe he could play on it, plead innocence, but all hope of doing so was shattered when Brent added, "And why the hell were you following those three?" Cap knew it was no use denying it, it was too obvious what he had been doing.

Brent gave him no time to answer, the answers needed to be given to Shorty and the others. Watching Cap carefully, his gun never wavering, Brent reached forward. "Your gun." Cap hesitated. "Give," snapped Brent. "Easy like," he added as a warning. Cap handed his gun over. Brent stuffed it into his belt and stepped to one side. He motioned with his gun. "Move," he ordered. Cap stepped past him, and Brent, with his Colt trained on Cap's back, fell in behind him.

They had gone about twenty yards when Cap heard a swoosh through the air followed by a dull sickening thud.

He spun round to see Brent keeling over, blood pouring from the side of his head, and Matt, holding the barrel of the rifle he had used as a club, watching Brent slump to the ground at his feet.

"What the . . . ?" gasped Cap. "How the hell d'you come to be here?"

"Long story," grinned Matt. "Seems a good job I was." His grin disappeared, leaving a frown. There was a touch of annoyance in his eyes as he stared hard at Cap. "But what the hell are you up to? What do you know about these hombres you're tailing that you wouldn't tell me? For some reason you didn't want me along today."

"Like you say, it's a long story," drawled Cap, then added appreciatively, "but, I'm mighty grateful you showed up." His tone changed to one charged with urgency. "Now, I want you to go back with the horses and wait for me."

"Not likely," snapped Matt. "You ain't getting rid of me as easily as that. You came to Two Rivers because of Doug's disappearance, so I figure following Clancey's troubleshooters has something to do with it. Doug was good to me, so if those bastards have done anything to him I want to be there."

Cap eyed Matt for a moment. He saw determination which would not be put off. Cap shrugged his shoulders but said nothing. If Matt learned things he didn't want to hear then so be it. If he was man enough he would surmount them. Cap bent down, retrieved his own gun, picked up Brent's and flung it among the rocks.

Cap straightened. "Right," he said. "Let's go." As he moved forward he indicated to the right. "I reckon if we use that way we can get close to the cave without being seen. Those three won't be expecting anyone so there'll be no lookout."

Matt nodded. "Ain't you telling me any more? You knew something yesterday, didn't you?" When Cap didn't answer he added, "I could tell there wasn't the same tension when I returned to the ranch."

"From what I learned by following Morrison to town, I felt pretty sure Doug was alive," said Cap.

"Why the hell didn't you tell me?" snapped Matt, his face clouding with annoyance.

"Easy," returned Cap. He wanted no tension in the youngster when they came face to face with Clancey's troubleshooters. "It was for your own good. If you knew I figured you'd want to ride with me today, and I didn't want you along."

"Well you've got me, like it or not," said an aggrieved Matt. "And I reckon it's a mighty good job I decided to check the valley out again."

"Sure is," smiled Cap. "Thanks." He slapped Matt appreciatively on the arm. "Now let's quit the talking and concentrate on what's ahead."

The two men, using all the cover they could, worked their way to the right so that they could approach the cave alongside the wall of rock. Reaching the rock face they paused a moment. Cap glanced queryingly at Matt, who nodded. Matt transferred his rifle to his left hand and drew his Colt with his right. Cap took his Colt from its holster.

Exercising extreme caution they inched their way towards the entrance to the cave. Voices became louder and by the time they were using the cover of a boulder close to the entrance they could hear quite clearly what was being said, for the unsuspecting men thought they had no need to keep their voices low. They were miles from anywhere, at the head of a hidden valley; no one could hear them.

"Come on, be sensible, Abe, you ain't going to get out of here unless you see things our way." The voice was sharp, incisive, with a touch of threat behind it.

Matt glanced at Cap. "Dutch Lowry," he mouthed silently.

Cap made no acknowledgement.

"Dutch is right, don't make things

harder on yourself." The voice paused for a slight moment then went on, "We want a settlement now. We ain't pussyfooting around any more. We mean to have our share of the money from Billings, no matter what."

Matt was starting to mouth the words Drew Rogers to Cap when the word Billings pierced his mind, lancing the past vividly before him. His mind raced. The last thing he had expected to hear. But what was this all about? What connection had Dutch Lowry and Drew Rogers with the raid? Dutch. Drew. Hell. Assumed names. They were Dutch Hardy and Drew Kinkaid. Killers. Killers of his ma and pa. Matt's mind exploded.

Cap saw Matt's face contort into a deadly mask of revenge. The calmness which had come to Matt's mind with the passage of time was suddenly swept away and replaced by that burning desire for justice, be it from the muzzle of a gun.

"That's why I didn't want you here,"

hissed Cap quietly. He stuck his Colt into Matt's ribs as a warning. "Don't do anything foolish to endanger Doug."

Matt's face darkened with angry frustration. The killers. He wanted those killers. Doug? He frowned. Cap had indicated that Doug was here. But what had he to do with Dutch and Drew?

"Drew, let me make him see reason." There was a sadistic note to the voice which Matt recognized as Shorty's.

"Hold on Shorty," said Drew. "Abe'll see reason, after all he rode with us and he knows we have a right to some of that Billings money. Abe, just sign the Circle C over to us; after all you must have bought it with the money from the bank raid, so part of it's really ours. We don't want a ranch so if, like you say, you ain't got cash to give us, you'd better hand over the ranch. We'll sell it to Clancey and then split with you."

Matt's mind tumbled with confusion. The Circle C bought with money from the Billings bank robbery. What the hell were these men talking about? Abe Reynolds was the man who got away from that raid but what had he to do with Circle C?

"And where does Shorty fit into this?"

Matt's mind pounded. That voice, the fourth voice, must belong to the man called Abe, but that was Doug's voice. Were Abe Reynolds and Doug Walters one and the same? They must be. Matt's thoughts whirled. The man he had grown to respect and admire, the man who had befriended him, was none other than Abe Reynolds, a member of the Fenton gang who had murdered his ma and pa. Doug was one of the men he had sworn to kill if ever he came across the survivors of the raid. That chance had been remote because he did not know what they looked like but now they were all here, the three who had escaped from Billings. Matt's confusion cleared enough for him to hear what was being said.

"... so Shorty drifted into Two Rivers, recognized you. He was in Billings the day of the robbery. He contacted us, hired us to Clancey, which made a perfect cover for us to size up the situation and then contact you. So you see if it hadn't been for Shorty we wouldn't be on the point of getting our rights. I reckon he deserves a cut of the money we get for the ranch."

Doug gave a derisive snort. "I know you two, you ain't going to split with Shorty, he's going to get my share and you're going to leave me here dead, where no one will find me. You'll think up some story to explain my disappearance after I've signed that paper. Well I ain't signing."

"Oh, you'll sign all right before we're through. We're fed up of trying to treat you right." The cold chill in Dutch's voice sent a shiver down Matt's spine. "You'll beg for a pen before we're through."

The dull thud of two blows coupled

with a wince of pain stiffened Matt. They were beating Doug. But why should he care, killers falling out, killers taking revenge, well let them. He felt the pressure of Cap's gun ease. He glanced at Doug's friend. Cap indicated with a slight inclination of the head that they should intervene.

Cap moved forward. Matt's pulse raced. Now he could get the murderers, now he could avenge his ma and pa. Cap paused just short of the entrance to the cave. He motioned his gun that he would move across the entrance and that Matt should take the near side. He waited a moment. Heard two more blows. Knew the men's attention would be rivetted on Doug.

He sprang forward and swivelled into a crouched position. In that moment he saw the three men swing round, their faces masks of amazement and confusion. Everything happened so swiftly and yet it seemed to come in slow motion.

Shorty's gun cleared leather. Cap

squeezed his trigger. Shorty staggered. He tried hard to raise his gun but the effort was too much. A glazed look of amazement clouded his eyes as he pitched to the ground. Cap flung himself sideways, bringing his gun round on Drew as he hit the ground, but Drew was already dropping to his knees, his face white and twisted. His gun fell from his grasp and he hit the ground face down. The cave reverberated with gunshots. Cap was aware of Dutch still on his feet, seeming to tower over everything. He caught a glimpse of Matt, his left arm oozing blood, right hand swinging his Colt from Drew to Dutch. Cap felt a sear across his forehead, and for a moment his senses dulled, then his mind seemed clearer than ever. Dutch was turning his gun on Matt when the bullet took him. Matt blazed again and again. Dutch's body jerked under the continuous impact which flung him backwards.

Matt's gun clicked on an empty

chamber. He flung it to one side and grabbed the rifle, which he had dropped when Drew's bullet took him in the arm. He scrambled to his feet, his mind pounding with only one thing, kill, kill, kill the killers. He strode to the prone body of Dutch and fired again. He stood for a moment, his chest heaving, drawing air into his lungs, then he turned to Doug.

All the anger, the hate he had spilled on Drew and Dutch in violent death was still there, still yearning to blaze forth on the last member of the Fenton gang. All the years between stood for nothing. Revenge still blazed in his mind. Justice, swift and sure. No namby-pambying with the law. Get it over and done with now!

He raised his rifle slowly on the helpless man, tied and trussed, his face bleeding from the blows he had been dealt.

Doug stared wide-eyed at the muzzle. His mind was still reeling under the tearing impact of crashing sound, now suddenly stilled, leaving his tormentors dead and himself facing a threatening rifle in the hands of a young man he cared about. The secret he had divulged only to his wife was out, known to Matt.

"Matt," Doug said quietly.

Matt paid no heed. He did not see Doug, the man who had been kind to him. He saw only his mother and father, dead before their time. He saw a gang who had left him an orphan.

Cap was on his feet. He had seen the look on Matt's face, a look he had seen before on men's faces when the killer instinct takes over and leaves them oblivious to anything else.

"Matt!" he screamed and flung himself at him. Cap's shoulder caught Matt's side and his arms clamped around his waist, tumbling him to the ground just as his finger closed around the trigger. The shot ricocheted harmlessly off the rocks. Cap released his grip on Matt. He twisted over, tore the rifle from Matt's grasp and slapped him hard in the face.

Matt jerked. His mind roared. For a split second he wanted to hit back but then the reality of the situation poured back, driving away the insane desire to kill which had gripped him in its soul-destroying vice.

His eyes focused on Cap who was kneeling over him. "Calm it, Matt." Cap's voice was firm and demanding.

Matt nodded. "I'm all right."

Cap pushed himself to his feet and felt the mark on his forehead where Dutch's bullet had come within an inch of killing him. He'd be all right. He stepped to Doug and quickly unfastened his bonds. "Thanks," Doug murmured. "I'm sure glad to see you." He rubbed his wrist as he scrambled to his feet, supported by Cap. He straightened and looked directly at Matt, who was watching him closely.

"So you know," said Doug softly.

Matt nodded. "Only a few minutes ago."

"Dorothy told me when she asked

for my help to find you. I tried to save him from the truth," said Cap, "but he followed me here." He gave a short laugh. "Just as well, he saved my life and no doubt yours."

"I suppose I did," mumbled Matt. "Those hombres wouldn't have let either of you out of here alive."

"And having saved you," went on Cap, "he was prepared to kill you."

"I was blinded by the past. Could only see my ma and pa," said Matt.

"I was no killer," said Doug, dabbing the blood on his face with his neckerchief. "I'd just joined the gang, wanted no part of killing. Dutch panicked."

"And the money?" queried Matt. "You bought the Circle C with it?"

Doug shook his head. "I returned the cash in exchange for freedom. The money for the Circle C came from elsewhere."

Matt nodded his understanding. He said no more but picked up his rifle. He looked hard at it. He glanced at Doug. The last of the Fenton gang.

It would be so easy to take him now, Cap's gun was back in its holster.

Cap knew what was roaring through Matt's mind, but he held away from the situation. A moment would make or break Matt. To interfere would leave Matt with doubts for the rest of his life. Doug knew it too. He waited.

Matt raised his rifle and emptied the bullets from it. They clattered on the rock. The tension broke.

"Let's go home, Matt," said Doug quietly. "I'll need someone to take over the ranch when I'm too old."

Other titles in the Linford Western Library:

TOP HAND
Wade Everett

The Broken T was big. But no ranch is big enough to let a man hide from himself.

GUN WOLVES OF LOBO BASIN
Lee Floren

The Feud was a blood debt. When Smoke Talbot found the outlaws who gunned down his folks he aimed to nail their hide to the barn door.

SHOTGUN SHARKEY
Marshall Grover

The westbound coach carrying the indomitable Larry and Stretch headed for a shooting showdown.

FIGHTING RAMROD
Charles N. Heckelmann

Most men would have cut their losses, but Frazer counted the bullets in his guns and said he'd soak the range in blood before he'd give up another inch of what was his.

LONE GUN
Eric Allen

Smoke Blackbird had been away too long. The Lequires had seized the Blackbird farm, forcing the Indians and settlers off, and no one seemed willing to fight! He had to fight alone.

THE THIRD RIDER
Barry Cord

Mel Rawlins wasn't going to let anything stand in his way. His father was murdered, his two brothers gone. Now Mel rode for vengeance.

ARIZONA DRIFTERS
W. C. Tuttle

When drifting Dutton and Lonnie Steelman decide to become partners they find that they have a common enemy in the formidable Thurston brothers.

TOMBSTONE
Matt Braun

Wells Fargo paid Luke Starbuck to outgun the silver-thieving stagecoach gang at Tombstone. Before long Luke can see the only thing bearing fruit in this eldorado will be the gallows tree.

HIGH BORDER RIDERS
Lee Floren

Buckshot McKee and Tortilla Joe cut the trail of a border tough who was running Mexican beef into Texas. They stopped the smuggler in his tracks.

BRETT RANDALL, GAMBLER
E. B. Mann

Larry Day had the choice of running away from the law or of assuming a dead man's place. No matter what he decided he was bound to end up dead.

THE GUNSHARP
William R. Cox

The Eggerleys weren't very smart. They trained their sights on Will Carney and Arizona's biggest blood bath began.

THE DEPUTY OF SAN RIANO
Lawrence A. Keating and
Al. P. Nelson

When a man fell dead from his horse, Ed Grant was spotted riding away from the scene. The deputy sheriff rode out after him and came up against everything from gunfire to dynamite.

FARGO: MASSACRE RIVER
John Benteen

The ambushers up ahead had now blocked the road. Fargo's convoy was a jumble, a perfect target for the insurgents' weapons!

SUNDANCE: DEATH IN THE LAVA
John Benteen

The Modoc's captured the wagon train and its cargo of gold. But now the halfbreed they called Sundance was going after it...

HARSH RECKONING
Phil Ketchum

Five years of keeping himself alive in a brutal prison had made Brand tough and careless about who he gunned down...